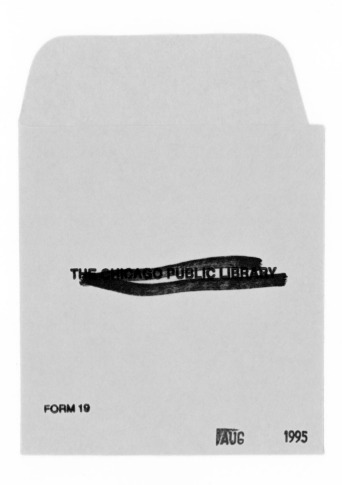

KNIGHT & DAY

KNIGHT & DAY

RON
NESSEN

AND

JOHANNA
NEUMAN

A TOM DOHERTY
ASSOCIATES BOOK
NEW YORK

KNIGHT & DAY

Copyright © 1995 by Ron Nessen and Johanna Neuman

This book is printed on acid-free paper.

A Forge Book
Published by Tom Doherty Associates, Inc.
175 Fifth Avenue
New York, N.Y. 10010

Forge® is a registered trademark of Tom Doherty Associates, Inc.

Library of Congress Cataloging-in-Publication Data

Nessen, Ron
    Knight & Day / Ron Nessen and Johanna Neuman
      p. cm.
    "A Tom Doherty Associates book."
    ISBN 0-312-85588-5
    I. Neuman, Johanna. II. Title.
  PS3564.E82K56 1995
  813' .54—dc20   95-2064
                                    CIP

First edition: May 1995

Printed in the United States of America
0 9 8 7 6 5 4 3 2 1

A NOTE TO THE READER:

This is a work of fiction. All of the characters and events portrayed in this novel are either products of the authors' imagination or are used fictitiously.

To Dr. Alvin Leeb,
an inspiration in courage

KNIGHT
& DAY

CHAPTER ONE

FIVE MINUTES TO midnight. Five minutes to airtime.

Jerry Knight went through his nightly ritual. He sipped hot tea from a mug, cleared his throat, and hummed up and down the scale to warm up his vocal cords.

"Testing. One, two, three. Testing. Stand by for God's gift to radio. Testing. One, two, three. Testing."

Sammy, the Vietnamese technician on the other side of the glass in the control room, grinned and gave him a thumbs-up. The host's microphone level was okay.

Jerry continued his preshow routine. He caught his reflection in the control-room glass, straightened his tie, smoothed back his hair. It was graying and thin but still not bad for a guy pushing fifty.

None of his two million listeners would see him, of course. And he wouldn't see them. That's what he liked about radio. He could be famous and anonymous at the same time. He could talk to millions of people every night without them knowing him or him knowing them.

The host studied his interview guest sitting across the baize-covered table. Curtis Davies Davenport, executive director of People to Save the Air. He promised to be one of those self-appointed, self-important Washington experts who think they possess the only solution to some perceived problem, and who denounce anyone with an opposing view as a fool or a crook or both.

Jerry hated this kind of guest, so intense, so smug, so humorless. The host looked over to K. T. Zorn, his producer, in the control room. He was sure K.T. had booked Davenport because she knew the guest would irritate him. And an irritated host was what Jerry's listeners tuned in to hear. He tried to catch K.T.'s eye to let her know he was on to her little scheme. But she pretended to be busy with her clipboard.

"Stand by. Ten seconds." The technician barked into Jerry's earphones.

Jerry took a final swallow of tea, cleared his throat again, hummed the scale one last time.

The hour hand, the minute hand, and the second hand of the studio clock aligned at 12.

The theme music blared from the speakers, a raucous rock melody. Sammy cranked up the volume on the music for a few seconds, then faded it down and brought in the announcer's recorded voice.

"It's midnight, and ATN, the All Talk Network, presents radio's most popular all-night talkmeister, Jerry Knight, and the *Night Talker* show, live from Washington, D.C. For the next five hours, sit back and listen while Jerry entertains, informs, and sometimes enrages you. If you're working, studying, or just having trouble sleeping, you are not alone. Ladies and gentlemen, here to keep you company all night is Jerry Knight, the Night Talker!"

The theme music swelled. The red ON AIR light on the studio wall lit up. Sammy pointed his finger at Jerry. Show time!

As always, the moment sent a jolt of energy through the host.

"Hello! Hello, you night people! You lucky night people. Lucky to be spending the night with the world's greatest living radio talk-show host. Certified the greatest. Ready, yet again, to go forth and do battle against the forces of political correctness, to puncture the windbags of the world, to throw buckets of cold water on the voluminous clouds of hot air emanating from this, your nation's capital."

CHAPTER TWO

JANE DAY JABBED a button on her bedside clock radio, cutting off Jerry Knight in mid-sentence. She changed the station to 97.1, light rock. Wimpy, but soothing for the midnight hour.

She couldn't stand Jerry Knight. Pompous, opinionated, opposed to everything she believed in, in favor of everything she abhorred. He made Pat Buchanan look like a charter member of the American Civil Liberties Union.

She wanted to listen to the show because one of her friends was going to be interviewed. But she couldn't stomach the Neanderthal host. Maybe she'd try again later.

In the meantime, a hot bubble bath and some snuggle time with her cat Bloomsbury seemed like the right prescription after a wearying day of work at the *Washington Post* capped by a night of celebratory drinking with her editor, Russ Williamson.

They had started at the Post Pub, a dark bar around the corner from the newspaper, and ended up at Twigs, in the

Capital Hilton at Sixteenth and K, where Russ had insisted on a nightcap.

There was much to celebrate. After days of digging and a lot of internal debate, the *Post* was finally going to run her exposé of Senator Barton Jacobsen. The conservative senator and presidential hopeful, a symbol of Republican rectitude, a leading advocate of traditional American values, had taken a payoff.

That's why it was so great to be a reporter in Washington. It was an equal-opportunity sleaze bucket. Not all officials were for sale. But most of them were for rent.

Jane hooked the security chain on her apartment door and checked to make sure she'd turned the two deadbolt locks. Her Adams-Morgan neighborhood was, as the real estate agents liked to say, in transition. Meaning: unsafe.

She hugged Bloomsbury and opened a can of tuna fish for him. It was his reward for being the only one who loved her and accepted her love without reservation or condition.

Of course Russ had tried to kiss her good night. But she'd sworn off married men. They always said they'd leave their wives. They never did.

Jane turned on the bathwater. While the tub filled, she stood naked in front of the tall mirror on the closet door and studied herself.

Ugh.

How was it possible to be scrawny everywhere except in her thighs? No more Häagen Dazs, she vowed, until she lost ten pounds.

She stared at her face. Using her fingers as scissors, she pretended to snip off the end of her needle nose. She was in one of those moods when she hated how she looked.

At least her eyes were okay. Green, almost the same color as Bloomsbury's.

And then there was her hair. It had been a bad hair day for Jane. But every day was a bad hair day for Jane, except for about a week in January when Washington's humidity was down around five percent.

Her hair wasn't auburn. It wasn't amber. It wasn't burnished copper. It didn't flame in the sun, driving men crazy. It was curly and almost orange. And the only one it drove crazy was Jane.

She stuffed her curls into a headwrap in the vain hope that the cloth would prevent the bathroom steam from making her hair even more curly.

Jane grimaced in the mirror. Maybe her fairy godmother would come in the night and give her gorgeous straight red hair. Or at least tame her curls so she looked like a Botticelli painting.

Doing her best Judy Tenuta imitation, she told the mirror, "It could happen."

CHAPTER THREE

O UR GUEST TONIGHT is Curtis Davies Davenport," Jerry Knight announced in a tone approaching a sneer. "He runs an outfit called People to Save the Air. Pretty big job, isn't it, Curtis, saving all that air?"

Davenport, a pale man, thirtysomething, with limp blond hair drooping over his forehead, stirred uneasily. He had known when he agreed to appear on the show that Knight would be critical. But Curtis figured it would give him a chance to deliver his clean-air message to a large audience. Still, this was a bit much.

"Yes, it is a big job," the guest ventured. "That's why we hope to recruit all Americans in our crusade against the internal combustion engine."

"Uh-huhhh!" Jerry snorted derisively. "A *crusade* against the internal combustion engine! D'ja hear that, all you Detroit auto workers? Curtis Davies Davenport and his fellow enviro-kooks want to do away with the automobile.

Do *away* with it! Think what *that's* going to do for your jobs out there in Detroit. Better check your neighborhood McDonald's. See if they've got any part-time jobs opening up."

"Really, Mr. Knight, that's not fair," Davenport protested.

"How'd you get to the studio tonight, Curtis?" Knight asked.

"How'd I get to the studio . . .?"

"Are these questions too hard for you, Curtis? Want me to use smaller words?"

"No, but—"

"You got here in a car, right?"

"Yes, I did."

"A black humongous, gas-guzzling, American-made, internal-combustion-engine *automobile*? Looks like it's got about thirty-five cylinders? With vanity license tags saying 'OURAIR'?"

Jerry had seen the car in the network parking garage. It was the latest confirmation of his belief that hypocrisy is Washington's major crop.

"I can explain," Davenport replied.

"Yes or no!" Jerry demanded.

"If you'll let me explain—"

"Yes or no!"

"Yes, but—"

"Never mind," Jerry said. "Subject two, the spotted owl. I believe you took part in the Save the Owls demonstration last weekend. You want to explain why you think it's more important to save the lives of a few flea-bitten rats with wings than it is to save the livelihoods of hardworking American loggers and their families?"

Davenport took a deep breath and warily began his explanation, anticipating that the nasty host would cut him off before he got very far.

"Extinction of a species is forever, Mr. Knight. We in the environmental movement believe that all species are created equal. Homo sapiens has no greater right to planet Earth's limited resources than any other species. Man has no right to eliminate the habitat—"

"Whoa!" Jerry interrupted. " 'All species are created equal'?" You mean those out-of-work logging workers up in Oregon are no better than skunks or cockroaches or mosquitoes? Is that what you're saying?"

"Well, in a sense—"

"I don't understand why one of those loggers who has worked in the woods all these years and is now forced to go on welfare doesn't come down to Washington and take a pop at you."

"Really—"

"We'll be back with your phone calls for the enviro-kook Curtis Davis Davenport after these messages."

Jerry cued Sammy to roll the commercials. The host hadn't been subtle. But he believed subtlety was lost on these self-absorbed fanatics. Anyhow, it was time to let his listeners in on the fun.

At two A.M., Davenport left, stunned by the barrage of hostile questions from Jerry and his fans.

The remaining three-hour segment of the show was known as Talk Back, America, during which the listeners called in to say whatever was on their minds. It was Jerry's favorite part of the program. All those anonymous voices from out of the darkness, confiding their problems, their fears, their prejudices, their gripes.

One caller, perturbed by Jerry's rough treatment of Davenport, accused the host of destroying the ozone layer by using underarm deodorant spray.

"It's better to smell bad than give the world skin cancer!" she screeched and hung up.

Another listener suggested that the Republicans could assure themselves of winning the White House by locating Elvis and running him for Vice President.

In the control room, K.T. grinned at Jerry. A lot of weirdos out there. Egged on by the biggest weirdo of them all. A weirdo with big ratings.

Finally, as five A.M. neared, K.T. held up one finger. One minute to sign-off. Jerry went into his closer.

"I leave you now, but in just nineteen short hours, I shall return to you, broadcasting live from Washington, D.C., home of the politics of bull, gathering place for the ideologically homeless, center of the universe for those with no fixed beliefs. But thanks to Jerry Knight, they shall not prevail! God bless you all, and God bless freedom!"

The theme music rose to a crescendo. The ON AIR light winked out. The *Night Talker* show was over.

Every morning, Jerry walked the two miles from the studio in downtown Washington to his penthouse apartment across the Potomac River in Rosslyn, Virginia. The streets were quiet at dawn. The bureaucrats, lawyers, and lobbyists weren't out yet, nor were the tourists, the street vendors, druggies, beggars, or whores. The streets were his.

Walking home was Jerry's only exercise, a time to come down from the adrenaline high he got from the broadcast. On his walk he usually smoked the one daily cigar his doctor allowed him. It was his chance to exhale billows of blue smoke without drawing the ire of the antismoking brigades.

Once home, Jerry scanned the *Post* while downing his

morning sleeping potion, two warm beers. A front-page story caught his eye.

An unnamed source had accused Senator Barton Jacobsen of accepting $100,000 for a secret presidential campaign fund after intervening with the EPA on behalf of the contributor.

Jerry knew Jacobsen and liked his staunch conservative views. He searched the story for more details. But they were skimpy.

"Damn *Post*," Jerry cursed aloud in the empty apartment. Doing a hatchet job on Jacobsen because he's a conservative. Probably trying to kill off his presidential chances. If he'd been a liberal and done the same thing, the story would have been buried in the want ad section. Or never would have been a story at all.

Jerry threw the paper aside, got into bed, and by six-thirty was asleep for the day.

CHAPTER FOUR

JANE DAY'S CLOCK radio went off at six-thirty A.M.

She normally lazed in bed a while, playing with Bloomsbury. But today she hopped up as soon as the music clicked on, eager to see how the *Post* had played her Jacobsen story. She pulled on a "Run for the Cure" sweatshirt and a pair of purple jogging shorts. She undid the locks on the door of her apartment and reached into the hall for the newspaper.

The reporter was momentarily disappointed to see that hers was not the lead story. That prized position, down the right side of page one, was filled by a piece about starvation in Somalia.

Her story ran down the left side, not bad placement for a reporter who normally wrote routine articles about environmental regulations. She smiled at her byline and the picture of Jacobsen. This was the first time she'd cracked the front page, territory usually reserved for the National and

Foreign desks, whose coterie of Pulitzer winners, TV panel-show regulars, and gigantic egos she dreamed of joining.

Jane had been tipped by a friend in the environmental movement that Z-Chem Plastics, a company in Jacobsen's home state of Indiana, had made a "loan" of $100,000 to a conservative policy study center that was actually a front to raise money for the senator's not-yet-announced presidential campaign.

The money had been paid after Jacobsen intervened with the Environmental Protection Agency to lessen a fine on Z-Chem for venting vast amounts of a toxic gas called HZCD-2L into the air.

Jane, with Russ's backing, had persuaded the editors to let her pursue the tip. And later, despite grumbling by one of the *Post*'s big-foot investigative reporters, Jane and Russ had persuaded the paper that she really had the goods on Jacobsen.

The most fun had been the phone call to Jacobsen at five P.M. the previous day, just before deadline, allowing him only enough time for a ritual denial, but not enough time for a detailed rebuttal.

She proudly reread her story now. She was relieved to see that the night editing crew had not made any last-minute changes.

"She shoots! She scores!" Jane said aloud.

She opened a can of Bloomsbury's favorite tuna-chicken dinner and set it on the floor of her tiny kitchen.

"Hi. I'm Jane. I'll be your server today."

The cat did not appear to be amused.

Jane picked up her Walkman and left the apartment for her morning jog.

Jane held her nose and breathed through her mouth as she stepped out of the building, but still she was enveloped in the stench of fresh urine. She wondered why the city didn't build public toilets for the homeless people who wandered her neighborhood.

Her radio was tuned to *All Things Considered,* the leisurely morning news and feature program on National Public Radio. She hoped the program would pick up her story. She knew many of the NPR reporters. They shared her loathing for the conservative Senator Jacobsen, especially since he had sponsored an amendment to cut off government funds for public broadcasting.

She headed north, up Eighteenth Street, past the run-down public tennis courts. A half-dozen homeless men were using the wall around the courts as a headboard.

"Hey, white girl," one of the men croaked at her. "Whyanya exercise on this?"

He groped inside the unbuttoned fly of his filthy pants. The other men cackled.

Someone threw an empty beer can in her direction.

Jane ran the gauntlet every morning. Each time it made her angry that the Reagan and Bush budget cuts had forced the men like these onto the streets. Since the eighties, society had turned heartless. Selfishness had become fashionable. And these were the victims.

After a few blocks, Eighteenth Street bent around to the left and turned into Calvert Street. Jane jogged past the chipping tan mosaic facade of the Calvert Cafe, a shabby Middle Eastern landmark that was a favorite with Washington's Lebanese community.

As she trotted across the Duke Ellington Bridge, some pig leaned out of a rusting Honda Civic and commented on her buns. She gave him the finger, sprinted across Connecticut Avenue, and descended into the bucolic paths of Rock Creek Park.

CHAPTER FIVE

JERRY KNIGHT WAS awakened by the phone. He pushed the black sleep mask up to his forehead and squinted at the digital clock on the bedside radio. Nine A.M.

The front desk knew not to put calls through during the day. Jerry fumbled for the phone.

"Yeah?"

"Sorry to disturb you, Mr. Knight. There's a police detective down here wants to talk to you."

"Tell him to come back at four o'clock."

"I told him you're sleeping. He says he gotta see you now."

"Shit. Send him up."

Jerry had worked the all-night shift for ten years. He was set in his routine and didn't like to have it upset. He cursed as he struggled into his silk paisley bathrobe, a gift from a recently departed girlfriend.

What the hell did a cop want him for at this hour? He

poured water and decaf beans into his Mr. Coffee.

Maybe someone had stolen his car from the apartment building's parking lot. Plenty of that going on. Damn kids. Parents didn't teach them respect for other people's property anymore.

Maybe something had happened to Lila. He smiled. Wouldn't that be nice! But unlikely. Ex-wives lived forever.

Or maybe it was his son Marty again. Jerry's smile faded.

The detective arrived at the door holding a badge in a leather case in one hand and a smudged business card in the other. Jerry, still fuzzy-headed from lack of sleep, took the card.

A. L. JONES

DETECTIVE

METROPOLITAN POLICE DEPARTMENT

HOMICIDE SQUAD

"What's the 'A.L.' stand for?" Even off the air, Jerry had a habit of interviewing people he met for the first time.

"Abraham Lincoln."

"Pardon?"

"A.L.—Abraham Lincoln Jones."

Jerry had never met anyone who looked less like Abraham Lincoln. The detective was short and squat, built along the lines of a fire hydrant. He was bald with a shaggy gray moustache and a day-old stubble of gray whiskers on his chin. And he was black. Well, actually a rich mahogany brown.

"Coffee?"

Jones nodded.

Jerry shuffled to the kitchen in his worn leather bedroom slippers and filled two mugs imprinted with the legend JERRY DOES IT ALL NIGHT.

When he returned to the living room, he found the detective admiring the view from the balcony of the penthouse. The view swept from the Gothic spires of Georgetown University and the yellow stone arches of the Francis Scott Key Bridge, past all the postcard monuments and memorials, to the regimented rows of white markers in Arlington Cemetery.

"Hmmm-uh!" the detective grunted approvingly. "You've got you some view here. I went to school a while to be an architect—"

"Detective Jones, I'd like to get back to sleep," Jerry interrupted. "I work all night."

"I know you do. I listen to you when I'm up late on a case."

Jones spoke in a deep baritone, slowly, as if he were weary.

"The front desk said you wanted to talk to me about something important . . .?"

Jones pulled a battered notebook from the pocket of his suit jacket.

"You know somebody named Curtis Davies Davenport?"

"I don't know him. I know who he is. He was a guest on my show last night."

"Yeah. That's what somebody told me."

"What's he done?"

"Ain't done nothing. Somebody killed him. Beat him to death in the parking garage next to your studio. Attendant found him when he came to work this morning."

"My God! That's awful."

"Yeah. You notice anything when you got in your car?"

"I don't park in the garage. I walk home."

Jones wrote that down.

"Anybody with him when he came up to the studio?"

"No. He was alone."

Jones wrote that down, too.

"Do you know who killed him?" Jerry asked the detective.

"Probably some drug boy. Needed a fix real bad, slammed Davenport, grabbed his wallet and watch to get some fast cash."

"What's the chance of catching him?"

"All depends what you mean by 'catch.' We identify a suspect in about half the homicides in D.C. But only about twenty-five percent get convicted of murder or manslaughter."

"I can't believe it. Killed right after he was on my show. And there's only a one-in-four chance the killer will be convicted? What the hell is our society coming to! I'm doing tonight's show on this outrage."

Jerry's outburst snapped the detective out of his lethargy.

"What are you getting so excited about, Mr. Night Talker? I don't hear you doing no programs about the couple hundred black people getting wasted every year in Washington. You wanna know what the hell our society's coming to? You go with me sometime. I'll show you what it's coming to. I'll show you a thirteen-year-old black boy shot in the head for the hundred-buck Nikes he bought with money he made selling crack. I'll show you a seventy-five-year-old grandmother accidentally got off the Metro at the wrong stop, had her throat slit for no reason at all. Almost five hundred people are dropped every year in D.C. and most of them are blacks busted by blacks. That's what the hell our society's coming to, Mr. Night Talker."

The detective's voice was hoarse. His brown face sagged with exhaustion.

"Come on my show tonight, Detective Jones, and talk about these things," Jerry urged. "It'll be great radio."

"Nah. I ain't no talker," the detective replied, sounding calmer but deeply tired. "You're the Night Talker. Anyhow, it ain't gonna do no good me talking about it. I've got to be out on the street. Maybe we can catch the motherfucker that busted Davenport."

CHAPTER SIX

J ANE DAY, SHOWERED and dressed after her morning jog, was just leaving her apartment when the phone rang.

"Hi, honey. How's my girl?"

"I'm great, Mom! I've got a big story in the paper today. Front page. Senator Jacobsen took a payoff to help a company in his state get off easy on pollution charges."

"No kidding. Sounds terrific. Will I see it in the *L.A. Times*?"

To her mother, if it wasn't in the *Los Angeles Times,* it wasn't news.

"It will be, Mom. Nobody else has the story yet. I broke it first."

"That's wonderful, honey. We're so proud of you."

Jane inspected herself in the hall mirror while she talked. She raked her fingers through her tangled orange hair, trying to make it straighter. Her fairy godmother had not shown up during the night. Again.

"It's early out there, Mom. How come you're calling so early? Is something wrong?"

"No, everything's fine. Your father had an early golf game, so I'm just puttering in the kitchen. I thought I'd call you and tell you the big news."

"What's the big news?"

Jane examined her nose in the mirror. Still long.

"Your cousin Debbie is having a baby! Isn't that exciting? She and Stan told the family last night. She's already three months pregnant. Aunt Susan and I are planning a baby shower and I want to schedule it when you can be here. What about Labor Day? No pun intended! You could come out for the long weekend."

"I don't know, Mom . . ."

Jane looked at Bloomsbury, who was stretched out indolently in a patch of sunshine, licking his front paw.

Cats had it easy. No family obligations.

"You'll have Labor Day off, honey."

"Yeah, probably," Jane concurred halfheartedly. "But I can't commit for sure right now. How about if you schedule it for Labor Day weekend, and I'll try to come. Okay?"

"Lovely, honey. That'll be great. Everybody wants to see you. By the way, are you seeing anybody?"

"Mom, please! I haven't got time for this today."

"I'm just asking."

"Okay. Yes, I'm seeing someone. Sometimes the President sneaks over here late at night after the First Lady is asleep. But other than that, there's nobody special."

There was a pause at the other end of the line. Then her mother gave a throaty laugh.

"You always were fresh."

"I love you, Mom," Jane said, laughing at her own joke. "But I've got to get to the newspaper. I'm late. I can't wait to find out what the reaction is to my Jacobsen story. And I'll probably have to write a follow-up piece."

"Okay. I love you, honey. Call me sometime!"

"Stop asking me if I'm seeing anybody, and I'll call you more often!"

The conversation left Jane depressed. In her subtle way, Mavis Day had once again chided her daughter for not settling down and getting married. After all, she was thirty-three. Look at Cousin Debbie, only twenty-two, already married and having a baby.

More mixed messages from Mom. She'd pushed Jane since childhood to succeed in a career. Now that Jane had fulfilled that set of aspirations, there was a whole new set to fulfill: marriage, kids, bone china, crystal, vacuum cleaners, and all the rest.

Well, maybe by Labor Day she would have someone to bring home for her mother's approval. Yeah, sure. Maybe George Stephanopoulos.

CHAPTER SEVEN

THE WALK FROM her Adams-Morgan apartment to the *Post* normally took Jane half an hour. But today, she moved at a brisk pace. She was eager to get to the paper and bask in the acclaim of her colleagues.

At nearly every corner, scruffy beggars held out their paper cups to her.

Jane had developed a policy about the homeless. Since she couldn't give to all of them, she had decided to give only to the beggars who enhanced the ambiance of the street—musicians, singers, mimes, and so forth. A friend denounced her for having a Dickensian attitude, requiring entertainment in return for her coins. But Jane argued that those who tried to create something had retained hope that should be encouraged.

Other people she knew had made similar choices about how to respond to the modern urban plague of begging. Her mother gave only to women. A friend gave at every third corner. Someone in the office gave gift certificates for McDonald's instead of money.

It was cruel to have to choose.

Even these urban realities could not dampen her spirits this morning, however. She turned her head at every *Washington Post* news rack to make sure her story was still there.

At the Fifteenth Street entrance to the newspaper, Jane waved to Jeremy, the security guard. Tourists were already lined up, waiting to look at the antique red linotype machine and walk past the newsroom, where daily they pointed through the glass partition at reporters and editors as if they were pandas at the zoo.

Jane got off the elevator at the fifth floor and headed across the vast newsroom to her cubicle. Not much on her voice mail. One message was from her friend Nellie, a reporter at the rival *Washington Times*, graciously acknowledging her clean hit on the Jacobsen story. Jane was about to scroll through the AP wire on her computer screen when Kirk Scoffield, the executive editor, slammed his hand down on her desk.

"Hell of a job, kid," he said in his gruff voice.

"Thanks, Mr. Scoffield. I appreciate the paper's confidence in me."

"That son of a bitch Jacobsen had it coming to him." Scoffield's leathery face crinkled into a sardonic grin. "Keep on his ass."

"I will!"

Jane's heart was beating hard as Scoffield walked away. He was a legend. The reporter who had been a friend of John Kennedy's. The editor who had faced down Richard Nixon. The editor who . . . liked her story!

She desperately needed caffeine.

At the coffee station, she encountered Wiley Saunders, one of the *Post*'s veteran congressional correspondents.

"Nice story," Wiley said. Jane thought his praise sounded grudging. These big feet always hate it when you scoop them on their own beat, she thought.

"Jacobsen's called a news conference at two o'clock to respond to your story," Saunders informed her. "I guess I'll take it from here."

"Not on your life," Jane protested. "I should cover the news conference. I know more about the Jacobsen story than anybody else."

Typical *Post* politics, she thought, bristling. Pulling rank to elbow her off her own story.

"Suit yourself." Saunders shrugged, stirring his coffee with his finger. "I just thought you'd want to be over at People to Save the Air. Wasn't Davenport a friend of yours?"

"Curtis is a friend of mine. What do you mean? What happened?"

"Davenport's dead," Saunders informed her in a sympathetic tone, realizing she hadn't heard the news yet. "Apparently killed by some druggie after he left the Jerry Knight show."

Jane felt dizzy. She grabbed a chair to keep from falling. She'd missed the news on NPR. Curtis was so earnest, so gentle. She couldn't imagine anyone killing him.

She ran to her computer and punched in the code for the local wire feed. She scrolled through the index. There it was. ENVIRONMENTALIST MURDER.

Curtis Davies Davenport, founder of the environmental organization People to Save the Air, was killed early Wednesday morning in the parking garage of a network radio studio shortly after he had been interviewed on the Jerry Knight show.

Police say he was killed by several blows to the head. Davenport's wallet and watch were taken in the apparent robbery. Police say the well-known environmentalist is the latest victim of Washington's epidemic of street violence.

The story went on to chronicle Davenport's career, his reputation for intelligence and probity, his gracious manner in handling Knight's tough questions in his final interview. The dispatch said Davenport was survived by his parents in Oregon and a sister in Colorado.

It sounded so cold in print.

CHAPTER EIGHT

T HE SETTING FOR Senator Jacobsen's news conference was the
Senate Caucus Room, an ornate chamber where many his-
toric events had transpired, most memorably Sam Ervin's
Watergate Hearings, which started the downfall of Richard
Nixon.

The room was already packed when Jane arrived fifteen
minutes before the scheduled start time. Wiley Saunders, the
Post's congressional correspondent, waved her to a seat he'd
saved for her in the front row.

Jane looked around. More than two hundred people
were crowded into the room, filling the hard chairs and
standing along the sides. Jane recognized some "name" correspondents from television.

The room was garishly illuminated by TV lights, giving
it the appearance of a stage set. At least ten minicams were
lined up at the back. A flock of photographers circled the
podium, measuring the light and adjusting their lenses.

They were all here because of her story, Jane thought. She felt people looking at her. It made her uneasy.

"Who are all these people?" she whispered to Wiley. "They're not all reporters."

"Staff, mostly," Wiley explained. "Looks like Jacobsen packed the place with supporters. But a lot of others came hoping to see his demise."

Waiting for the news conference to begin, Jane pulled that morning's *Post* from her huge tapestry shoulder bag and anxiously reread her story. What would Jacobsen say about it? she worried.

Suddenly there was a flurry at the side door, setting off a cacophony of motorized cameras.

The senator strode in smiling, followed by his wife, Marie, his press secretary, Judy Anselmo, and his chief of staff, Jack VanDyke.

Most of the audience burst into applause. Wiley was right. Jacobsen had packed the house.

He was a tall man, a couple of inches over six feet, exuding power and confidence. A craggy face. Silvery hair, stylishly long, carefully trimmed, fluffed, and sprayed. He wore a perfectly tailored charcoal gray suit that emphasized his broad shoulders and trim waist. Light gray shirt with contrasting white collar and French cuffs. Red tie, not too bright.

Well, he certainly looks like a presidential candidate, Jane thought. Her eyes followed Jacobsen as he moved to the podium, Marie one step behind him. He must be worried about his hopes for the presidency, Jane thought, to bring out the wife. The senator put on a pair of silver-rimmed eyeglasses, withdrew a statement from his inside jacket pocket, took a deep breath, and read.

"For the past twenty-two years, I have been honored to

serve the American people, first as mayor of my hometown, then in the House of Representatives, and now in the United States Senate." Jacobsen's voice was surprisingly high-pitched, edged with a Midwestern flatness.

"This morning I awoke to find those twenty-two years of public service stained and tarnished by an allegation in the *Washington Post* that I accepted an illegal campaign contribution in return for 'fixing'—that's the word that was used—for 'fixing' a case before the Environmental Protection Agency. Let me be very, very clear. I totally and categorically deny that allegation."

Jane was surprised by his flat denial.

She had expected one of the mealymouthed excuses public officials typically offer when caught misbehaving: "I have no recollection"; "An overzealous staff member did it"; "All of us, I'm sure, committed youthful indiscretions"; or the nonspecific "Mistakes were made."

An unequivocal denial was rare.

"I notice that the name of the person making this allegation against me is not identified anywhere in the story," Jacobsen continued. "Inside the Beltway, we call that person 'an anonymous source.' Where I come from, out in the real America, we call that person a coward. Or a polecat."

Jacobsen scanned the audience until he found Jane. He glared at her. One of the photographers turned away from the podium and clicked off a few shots of her. She felt her face redden.

"It is not accidental that this false charge against me was published now," Jacobsen read from his statement. "I think you may know that some of my friends are urging me to explore the possibility of running for President of these great United States."

He grinned guilelessly and a ripple of laughter ran

through the audience.

"If the *Washington Post* and the liberal politicians and interest groups it represents think these shabby tactics will knock me out of the race or silence my ideas, they've got another think coming!"

He raised his voice and hit the podium with his fist.

His supporters applauded.

"The American people are tired of this kind of mudslinging. They are tired of this kind of negative politics. They are desperately seeking a return to civility in our politics and in our country. They are seeking a return to the conservative values that made this country great in the first place. That's what I stand for. That's the crusade I intend to lead. I will not be deterred. I will not be smeared."

More applause.

Jacobsen looked down at his statement.

"I am confident that when this false accusation is fully examined, I will be exonerated. In the meantime, I am fortunate to have the loving support of my wife, Marie."

On cue, she stepped forward. She looked ten years older than her husband. Tears glistened in her eyes. Marie took his hand, and kissed him on the cheek.

"Marie! I didn't know this was going to be an X-rated news conference!"

His fans chuckled appreciatively.

"I will get through this because of Marie, and the wonderful support of the American people, and because of my faith in God."

More applause.

"I want to conclude by announcing that I have sent a letter this morning to the *Washington Post,* to Mr. Kirk Scoffield, the executive editor, asking for a retraction of the story. Now, I will try to answer your questions."

Jane was scared.

Her first big story and it seemed to have blown up in her face.

The reporters shouted hysterically for Jacobsen to recognize them.

"Senator! Senator!"

With a look of amusement, he let the feeding frenzy rage unchecked for a few moments. It was a tactic he often employed. It made him look calm and in control, in contrast to the baying of the quarrelsome journalists.

The reporters' questions fell into two rough categories: snarled queries from reporters trying to extract enough damaging quotes to match without any real investigating the story Jane had been working on for days, and suck-up questions from reporters who hoped to win favor with a possible future President.

When Jacobsen had first come to the Senate, his press secretary had hired a PR agency to put him through two days of videotaped media training. He'd learned the lessons well. Make two or three simple points over and over again. Restate questions, then answer your own version, not the reporter's. Never leave a false premise uncorrected. And don't say anything you don't want to see ripped out of context and standing alone as a soundbite on the nightly news.

Had Jacobsen's presidential campaign committee accepted a $100,000 loan from Z-Chem?

He had no presidential campaign committee, at the moment. Perhaps Z-Chem had made a perfectly proper contribution or loan to the policy research organization called the Center for the Advancement of Conservative Value Initiatives, of which he had the honor to serve as chairman. The reporter needed to check with the people who handle finances for the center.

"Let me answer that one right now, Senator." Jack VanDyke, his chief of staff, stepped forward. Jacobsen gave way at the podium.

VanDyke had the reputation of being a mean political operative. He didn't like reporters much, and he glowered at them now.

"I'm the treasurer of the center," VanDyke announced. "Yeah, Z-Chem made a loan to get the center started. It's perfectly legal. I signed a note for the money. We intend to pay back every penny once the contributions start coming in. Senator Jacobsen is not involved in the finances. He knew nothing about this loan. Anybody says he did know is a damn liar. I accept full responsibility."

The aide relinquished the podium to Jacobsen.

"Taking a bullet for the chief," a reporter in the second row commented in a stage whisper. The other reporters laughed, then resumed their questioning of the senator. Had he used his influence to persuade the EPA to drop charges that Z-Chem regularly released a toxic gas called HZCD-2L into the air from its plastics plant?

His office devoted a good deal of time and effort to helping the good people of his state deal with the mindless and mind-boggling federal bureaucracy. Missing Social Security checks. Difficulties gaining admission to VA hospitals. Scholarships for worthy minority youngsters. That kind of thing. Z-Chem was a large employer in his state. So it would be natural for his staff to help the company and its thousands of workers to present their case to a federal regulatory agency.

But wasn't there a quid pro quo? Didn't Jacobsen fix things for Z-Chem in return for a $100,000 payoff?

He never let them get under his skin, never stopped smiling, never stopped being charming.

Perhaps the questioner was at the wrong news conference. He must be looking for the Keating Five.

Another lesson from the media trainer. Turn aside tough questions with humor.

"But *was* there a quid pro quo?" Jane heard herself ask, almost without realizing she was speaking.

"I think Jack has answered that one already, Miss Day," Jacobsen replied, smiling. He quickly turned and pointed to another questioner before she could pursue it.

When the questioning became repetitious, Jane slipped out, found a phone booth, and called Russ Williamson at the newspaper.

She started to recount what Jacobsen had said.

"I saw it on CNN," Williamson interrupted her. "We've got a problem. You better get back here."

"The denial—"

"We'll talk about it when you get here." He hung up.

By the time she returned to the caucus room, the news conference was over. The TV crews were packing their equipment. Most of the reporters had gone off to write their stories. A few remained, gathered around Jack VanDyke, Jacobsen's chief of staff.

He was spinning them, in Washington parlance, reinforcing and expanding on what the senator had said, adding background, offering supporting interpretations, trying to sell them on his version of the episode.

Jane approached the circle of reporters.

VanDyke stopped his spinning when he saw her.

"You got your tit caught in a wringer, lady," he sneered.

CHAPTER NINE

JANE KNEW IT was going to be bad when Russ waved her into one of the conference rooms rimming the newsroom instead of chewing her out at his desk.

She waited silently as the others gathered. Russ. Kirk Scoffield. And a man she didn't recognize. Everyone seemed tense.

"Jacobsen denies your story," Scoffield began without preamble.

"I think my story—" Jane started.

"I don't give a shit what you think!" Scoffield interrupted, slamming his fist down on the table. "I want proof, sources, facts. This newspaper had one Janet Cooke and I'll be goddamn if it's going to have another one on my watch."

Jane explained that campaign finance rules were ambiguous. Scoffield didn't interrupt, but she could tell he was barely containing himself.

She told them she'd confirmed that Z-Chem had given

$100,000 to the Center for the Advancement of Conservative Value Initiatives. She'd seen the records. The money was there.

"And everybody knows the center is a front for Jacobsen's presidential campaign," she declared.

" 'Everybody knows'?" Scoffield cut her off. " 'Everybody knows'? That doesn't pass for facts on this newspaper."

She was trying to keep her head. She told them she had copies of EPA records showing that a tough penalty for pumping toxic gas into the atmosphere had first been imposed on Z-Chem, and then mysteriously withdrawn for a more lenient fine.

"And the EPA did that because Jacobsen intervened?" Scoffield asked. "And he intervened because Z-Chem lent $100,000 to a front for his presidential campaign?"

"That's what my source tells me," Jane said firmly.

Scoffield and Russ Williamson exchanged looks.

"What do you think, Lofton?" Scoffield asked the third man.

Jane realized he was Lofton Mizell, one of the *Post*'s lawyers.

"Weak," the lawyer pronounced. "There's no reason to believe the loan to the think tank was illegal. The EPA often modifies its enforcement actions after senior officials review them. And the allegation that Jacobsen intervened at the EPA because of the loan comes from an unidentified source."

"The story doesn't say Jacobsen threw his weight around at the EPA *because* of the loan," Jane protested.

"But you *implied* it," Russ retorted angrily. "You led me to believe that your source had the goods on Jacobsen."

Jane realized Russ wasn't going to protect her. He was covering his own ass with Scoffield. She was on her own.

"The story was premature," Scoffield declared, glaring at Russ. "It was not fully researched when you put it in the paper. But I am not going to run a goddamn retraction for that right-wing son of a bitch. Jacobsen and the conservatives would never stop rubbing our nose in it if we did."

He got up and paced. A glass wall separated the conference room from the newsroom. Jane had the feeling everyone out there was staring at this scene.

"Here's how we get out of it," Scoffield announced.

"You go back to your source," he instructed Jane. "You get more details, dates, times, names, when Jacobsen contacted the EPA. Also, you get your source to make a solid connection between the money and Jacobsen leaning on the EPA. Documents, if the source can get them."

Scoffield turned on Russ Williamson.

"And this time you go over her copy with a goddamn fine-tooth comb, make sure she's got the *whole* story. All the facts. All the questions answered. Understand?"

"I never would have run the story, Kirk, if she hadn't assured me she had it cold," Russ protested weakly.

"I can't go back to my source," Jane said quietly.

"Why not?" Scoffield asked.

"Because my source is dead."

"Dead?"

"My source was Curtis Davenport. He was killed this morning in a robbery on M Street. I can't get any more details from him."

She sat stiffly. She was not going to let them see her cry.

The conference room was still.

"Go back to your desk," Scoffield ordered her. "Russ will tell you what we decide."

She went to the women's rest room and threw up her

lunch. Then she went to her desk and waited. After fifteen minutes, Russ appeared.

The paper would run a "clarification," saying it never intended to imply that Senator Jacobsen had done anything illegal, and that it regretted any inconvenience such an inference may have caused.

She was demoted to the Metro section, mostly police stuff.

Her first assignment would be the investigation of Curtis's death.

She didn't say anything.

"I tried to save you, Jane," Russ lied. "I really did."

CHAPTER TEN

THE NIGHT AFTER Davenport's murder, K. T. Zorn was already at the studio when Jerry arrived an hour before show time.

The producer never seemed to go home. She was there when he left at dawn and there when he came back at night. In fact, she did go home and sleep during the day, leaving Rosanne the Booker to line up each night's guests according to K.T.'s instructions.

After the disturbing visit from Detective Jones, Jerry had phoned Roseanne and ordered her to cancel that night's scheduled guest and to arrange a show on Washington crime. She had corralled the police chief, a black gang member who wanted to be identified only as Bad Bro, a gun-control advocate, and the head of an organization that campaigned to send convicted criminals to music camps instead of prison.

Jerry would amply represent the law-and-order view-point.

He was in a grumpy mood. He hadn't been able to sleep well after Detective Jones had left. And a boxed item he found on page three of K.T.'s early edition of the next day's *Post* didn't improve his frame of mind.

"They ought to be ashamed of themselves!" Jerry thundered.

"What is it now?" K.T. asked in a tone she might use with an irksome child. She was used to the host's tirades, especially when he was reading the *Washington Post*.

"First they smear Jacobsen because he's a conservative," Jerry said. "Then when he calls them on it and they can't back up their hatchet job, they bury a half-ass retraction where no one will see it."

K.T. rolled her eyes and continued to scribble on the yellow legal pad clamped to her ever-present clipboard.

K.T.'s iron gray hair was clipped in a crew cut, except for a ruff of slightly longer hair framing her forehead. She was short, less than five feet. A gray sweater and long paisley skirt emphasized her lithe figure.

Jerry had come on to her when she was first hired, as he did with most women he encountered. She'd made it clear that he was the wrong gender for her. After that, they'd gotten along famously.

Jerry read the *Post*'s front-page coverage of the Davenport murder, scowling at the references to him "grilling" the victim in his last interview. No suspects had been arrested. And probably never would be, Jerry assumed. D.C. cops were great at giving parking tickets. Catching murderers? Zero.

Next, the host turned his attention to a pile of hate

mail. Reading the vile letters always seemed to exhilarate him, charging him up for the program. He wore the denunciations like badges of honor.

"Listen to this," he commanded K.T.

" 'Dear Adolf Hitler . . .' Why the hell do they equate my views with Hitler's? Why don't they write 'Dear Winston Churchill'? That would be more in keeping with my contribution to an enlightened public dialogue."

K.T. ignored him. She'd previously worked for Phil Donahue, the *Today* show, and Rush Limbaugh. Nothing any of these egomaniacs said fazed her. She had an exceedingly serene personality.

"Want to hear something interesting?" K.T. asked.

"Hmmm." Jerry was preoccupied with his hate mail.

"I took a phone call for Davenport before he went on the air last night."

"Really?" Jerry put down the letters. She had his attention. "Who was it?"

"The guy wouldn't give his name, just said it was important that he talk to Davenport. He left a number. See?" She pulled a wrinkled pink message form from her sweater pocket. "I dug it out of the trash can after I heard about Davenport's murder."

"It's a 224 number. That's the Senate."

"Yep."

"Did Davenport return the call?"

"I think so. I gave him the message and he said he wanted to make a call in private. So I let him use one of the offices."

"Maybe it's just a coincidence."

"And maybe it's not."

"The cops say it was just a random street crime."

"There's a historic first," K.T. said. "Correct me if I'm

wrong, but I believe that's the first time you've ever accepted the word of the D.C. cops."

"It wouldn't be so unusual for Davenport to get a call from the Hill," Jerry said. "He must have known a lot of senators and staff people. Seems like he was up there every week testifying in favor of saving the air, saving the whales, saving the trees. Every damn thing except saving the taxpayers money."

"So you're going to buy the cops' version?"

"I'll phone that detective who came to see me and tell him about the call. Let him find out if it's connected. That way, my conscience is clear. I've performed my duty as a law-abiding citizen."

Jerry left a message for A. L. Jones at the number on his card. Twenty minutes later he got a call back from the detective.

"Sorry to wake you up," Jerry said.

"You didn't wake me up," Jones rumbled. "I been out on 295. Woman driving home from her wedding party got shot by somebody pulled up next to her. Hit her baby, too."

"Jesus! I'm leading the show with that tonight!"

"Whatja call about?" Jones asked in his weary baritone.

"I have something that might help you with the Davenport case."

"Yeah?"

Jerry got the feeling the detective was concentrating on something else at the other end of the line.

"Davenport got a strange phone call just before he went on the show last night."

"Uh-huh."

"Maybe it was connected to his murder."

There was no response from Jones. Now Jerry was sure the detective was concentrating on something else.

"Hello? Hello? Anybody there?" Jerry prodded sarcastically.

"What time you get off?" Jones asked. "Five?"

"Right."

"I'll come up there."

CHAPTER ELEVEN

Y OU DIDN'T GET much sleep," Jerry greeted the detective
when he arrived in the control room shortly after five A.M.

"Didn't get *no* sleep," Jones replied. "Trying to find out
who busted that woman on 295."

"Any suspects?" Jerry went into his interview mode.

"Nah. Couple of drivers saw it. But they're afraid to
talk."

"Can't you make them talk?" Jerry asked.

"Make 'em?" The detective snorted. "Man, you can't
make people sign their own death warrant. Lot of people
who see shootings, and talk about it, get shot themselves.
Word gets around real fast. I've lost witnesses. We tell 'em
we'll protect 'em. But we can't."

He sounded tired and discouraged.

"Want breakfast?" the detective asked.

"Sure."

Jones's dirty white Ford was parked at the curb in front

of the ATN building. It was obviously an unmarked police car. Nobody but the police department would buy a car that inconspicuous.

The inside of the car was littered with McDonald's wrappers, empty root beer cans, plastic audio cassettes, a bundle of dirty shirts, and, inexplicably, an oversized Prince tennis racket. The detective offered no explanation or apology for the condition of his vehicle.

Jerry swept debris off the passenger seat and got in.

Jones wheeled up Connecticut Avenue. There was almost no traffic at that hour. The posh shops that lined the avenue were still dark, and the street vendors had not yet set up their sidewalk bazaars.

The only signs of life were the stirrings of the homeless sleeping in the doorways of the posh shops.

"How can you stand all the killing that goes on in this city?" Jerry asked as they drove through the underpass beneath Dupont Circle.

"I spent two tours in Nam," Jones growled. "Sometimes I think this is worse. Used to be, when I first went on Homicide, most of the cases were 'wife killed the husband for cheating on her,' 'somebody killed somebody owed him money.' Now, you look at somebody the wrong way, he whips out a Nine and drops you. Then, your friend drops him. Then his friend drops your friend, and on and on."

"They let too damn many of 'em off," Jerry said.

The detective nodded his agreement.

"Probation. Parole. Halfway houses. Treatment centers. Juvenile Village. Half the time we don't catch 'em in the first place. And when we do catch 'em, half the time the witnesses are too scared to testify against 'em anyway."

"The parents don't teach them to respect the sanctity of human life," Jerry declared.

Jones didn't challenge that assertion.

The massive Washington Hilton loomed on the right.

Jones swung the car right onto Columbia Road, a street once as elegant as Park Avenue. Over the years, though, Adams-Morgan had deteriorated. Now it was home to an uneasy mix of aging sixties people, ambitious nineties people, assertive gays, newly arrived Hispanics, and struggling blacks.

"This is it," the detective announced as he pulled to a stop in front of the all-night 7-Eleven in Adams-Morgan.

"Big entertainment budget they give you," Jerry joked.

"Yeah, *real* big." Jones grinned. "The manager here gives free coffee and food to policemen. So there's usually a cruiser or two parked outside. People who live around here like it. It discourages the bad guys. I've seen people from the neighborhood run over to the 7-Eleven when they need help because they know there's almost always a cop here. It's faster than dialing 911."

The Asian cashier greeted Jones by name. The detective ordered two glazed doughnuts. He poured coffee into a large paper cup, adding cream and three packets of sugar. Jerry settled for one doughnut and a decaf.

"I hope you don't mind eating in the car," Jones said as he led the way back to his unmarked cruiser. "The car's my living room, dining room, office, just about everything."

They laid their doughnuts out in the waxed-paper wrappings on the center armrest. Jerry set his coffee cup on the dashboard where it steamed a circle on the windshield. The detective bit a triangular hole in the lid of his cup and spit the bits of plastic onto the floor.

"Tell me about the phone call Davenport got," Jones asked after taking his first sip of coffee.

"I wasn't there myself," Jerry explained. "K.T. . . . . K. T.

Zorn, my producer, took the call. The caller wouldn't leave a name, but he said it was important to talk to Davenport, and he left a phone number."

"Uh-huh. Then what?"

"That's it. K.T. assumes Davenport returned the call. But she doesn't know who it was from or what it was about."

To Jones, detective work was like putting together a jigsaw puzzle. Try to fit the pieces together. See which ones made a picture. When you put the pieces together in the right combination you solved the murder.

But he couldn't see how the phone call fit into the puzzle of Davenport's murder. It didn't seem like a puzzle piece at all.

"Doesn't sound like the call had anything to do with whoever dropped Davenport," the detective said.

"But the call was from a 224 number," Jerry persisted. "That means it was from a phone at the U.S. Senate."

"So what?" Jones replied. "Wasn't Davenport a big deal, testifying all the time about that environmental shit? And I hear he had a girlfriend worked on the Hill."

"You're not even going to check out the call?" Jerry shook his head.

"This ain't the *Columbo* show, man," Jones said. "This is Washington, D.C. People kill other people every day for a few bucks. Or for no reason at all. Davenport was in the wrong place at the wrong time. That's all. The dude was dropped for his money by some fool hard up for a fix. Happens all the time."

"I don't know which is worse, that your theory is probably right or that you won't even entertain the idea that it might not be right."

"Hey, man." The detective's deep rumble went up a

half-octave. "I don't need none of your 'cops ain't worth shit' routine this morning."

They sat in silence a while.

"Listen, man. I heard a tape of your show. You gave Davenport a hard time." The detective took a large bite of doughnut.

"I give most of my guests a hard time, especially the ones with a high bullshit quotient."

"I thought that routine of yours every night was just jivin' for the listeners. Sounds like maybe them rough questions wasn't no act."

"Why'd you bring up my interview with Davenport?"

"Maybe somebody heard your show, got riled up at Davenport, and waited for him in the garage. You practically invited—what did you call 'em?—lumberjacks, loggers to take a pop at him."

"Nobody kills anybody in Washington over political differences," Jerry replied. "Character assassination, maybe. But not real murder."

A chuckle rumbled deep in the detective's chest.

"Character assassination. Yeah."

"You don't really believe my interview incited someone to come after Davenport, do you?"

"Nah," Jones chuckled again. "I'm just pulling your chain."

"You have a strange sense of humor, Detective."

"You, too."

They sat sipping coffee and munching doughnuts.

"How long you got in?" Jerry asked.

"Eighteen years. Seven in homicide."

"Jesus!"

Jones couldn't tell whether Jerry's exclamation meant the white man thought he was a hero or a fool.

"How long you need in to retire?"

"Twenty."

"You'll quit then?" Jerry sounded as though he were conducting an interview in the *Night Talker* studio instead of sitting in a detective's car eating doughnuts in front of a 7-Eleven in Adams-Morgan.

"I don't know. Maybe. I've got friends got out, went into security work, making three times what I'm making. But I don't know. I feel some kind of obligation to this place. I was *born* in D.C. I feel like I've got to do what I can do . . . you know . . . Shit! You got me talking trash!"

Jones normally kept his thoughts to himself. But the fatique and depression he felt had loosened his tongue.

"Is there a Mrs. A. L. Jones?" Jerry asked.

"There *was,*" the detective responded. "But she left. Didn't like my hours. Said I was 'difficult to live with.' She's up in New Jersey. Nursing supervisor. Married a doctor. I *am* difficult to live with. But I don't see why she couldn't get used to me."

The detective drained the last of his coffee.

"You married?" he asked Jerry.

"Have been. A couple of times."

"Yeah, like five or six, I read somewhere."

"Only three!" Jerry insisted.

"Can't live with 'em, can't live without 'em."

Jones chuckled deep in his chest again. He crumpled the waxed-paper wrappings, stuffed them into his empty paper cup, and flipped it onto the litter in the back.

"I'll drive you home." Jones started the Ford. "Past your bedtime."

CHAPTER TWELVE

As JERRY UNDRESSED for bed, he discovered K.T.'s pink message slip, recording the mysterious call to Davenport, stuffed in his pants pocket.

The conversation with Jones had reinforced Jerry's conviction that the detective was unlikely to find Davenport's murderer. Jones was unwilling to even consider the possibility that the killing might not have been just a random street crime.

Jerry decided to trace the phone number himself.

Six forty-five. Too early to call a Senate number.

So he dialed the number on the pink message form when he woke up in the afternoon.

"Mr. VanDyke's office," a secretary's voice answered.

"Whose office is this?"

"This is Mr. VanDyke's office. Who's calling?"

"Sorry. I must have the wrong number."

Jerry hung up. The name sounded familiar. He padded

into his den and consulted a white-bound *Congressional Directory.*

The index showed two VanDykes, Emily W. and James T. He turned to the page reference for James T.

Now he placed the name.

Jack VanDyke, hard-eyed, win-at-all-costs political operative in the mold of Lee Atwater.

Official title: Chief of Staff to Senator Barton Jacobsen.

CHAPTER THIRTEEN

P HONE CALL FOR you, Jerry," K.T. advised the talk-show host as he left the studio at five A.M. after another night of trodding down the downtrodden and comforting the comfortable, as he liked to put it.

"Show's over. Tell 'em to call back tonight."

"It's not a listener."

Jerry jabbed the flashing button on the phone at the producer's console.

"Hello?"

"Where's my money!"

"It's The Bitch," Jerry silently mouthed to K.T. She nodded and ducked back to her clipboard. He didn't have to identify the caller. K.T. knew it was Jerry's ex-wife Lila.

"Lila, what are you doing up at this hour? Did your coven go on an all-night broom ride?"

"Where the fuck's my money!"

"It's the first of the month, Lila. I mailed your check yesterday, just like I'm supposed to."

"You're full of shit!"

"And you're full of booze."

"What did you say!"

"I said take a snooze. The check should be delivered today."

"It better be!"

Lila had a habit that irritated Jerry when they were married but amused him now. When she was angry and/or drunk, her decibel level rose higher and higher with each sentence. Jerry had started the conversation with the phone to his ear. As she got louder, he held the phone away from his ear. Now he was holding it at arm's length and he could still hear her. He could picture Lila in their old house in Chevy Chase, her face turning purple, spittle forming in the corners of her mouth, spraying the mouthpiece with each angry word.

K.T. giggled at the incredibly loud voice coming out of the phone, and that made Jerry giggle.

"Don't laugh at me, you bastard! If that check's not here today, I'm calling *People* magazine and telling them I've got to go on welfare because you won't give me any money!"

"Even under the liberals, I don't think you qualify for welfare, Lila. I pay you five thousand dollars a month."

"And how much do you pay that bimbo you're sleeping with!"

"Have a nice day," Jerry said, and hung up.

He went to his office and leafed through the *Post*. He found a three-paragraph story on Davenport's murder in the Metro section. Nothing new. Police had no suspects. Plans were being made for a memorial service.

"Hey, K.T.," Jerry shouted through the wall to the producer in the next office. "Feel like going to a reception with me tonight?"

"Which reception?"

"I don't know yet."

K.T. rolled her eyes. These guys were impossible. Maybe she should try working for Oprah.

"I'm looking for a reception where we're likely to run into Jack VanDyke."

"The Jeffrey Dahmer of American politics? Okay, I'll play straight man. 'And why do you want to run into Jack VanDyke?' "

"I traced the phone call Davenport received just before the show to VanDyke's office."

"Yeah?"

"Yeah. Detective Jones has no interest in checking out the call. So I'm going to ask VanDyke myself why he called Davenport the night of the murder."

"Are you playing amateur detective?" K.T. laughed. "You've never once guessed the killer on *Murder She Wrote.*"

Jerry didn't know why he wanted to confront VanDyke. Jones's joking suggestion that the host's treatment of Davenport might have incited a listener to ambush the guest troubled him. Although the detective had later laughed off the idea, he had planted a seed of doubt. Jerry didn't feel responsible for his guest's death. But he did feel involved.

Jerry punched keys on his computer until the Associated Press Daybook appeared on the screen, listing all the events scheduled in Washington that day. He knew that VanDyke was a regular rider on the cocktail-party circuit, often hitting a half-dozen parties in an evening, picking up gossip, spreading poison about his enemies, imbibing useful information while others imbibed gin.

Jerry found a listing for an event he thought VanDyke

would find difficult to pass up. The Committee to Instill Family Values Through School Prayer. A reception at six P.M. at the J. W. Marriott Hotel, Fourteenth and Pennsylvania Avenue, the Capitol Ballroom, Foyer B.

Jerry got up from his desk.

"I'm going home and get a good day's sleep," he told K.T. "I'll pick you up at five-thirty."

"I don't know what I did to deserve this honor," she replied.

CHAPTER FOURTEEN

No one ever showed up at a Washington reception until at least forty-five minutes past the announced start time. It was a way of letting the other attendees know that your work—at the Capitol, at the law firm, at the network—was too important to break away for something as frivolous as a party.

So Jerry figured he had plenty of time to pick up K.T. and get to the Marriott in time to be fashionably late.

But as they drove across Memorial Bridge into Washington, traffic was suddenly blocked by a demonstration.

"What the hell is *this* all about?" Jerry demanded. He flicked on the car's automatic door locks.

"Looks like FUTS," replied K.T., reading the demonstrators' banners.

"Those damn enviro-kooks!" Jerry leaned on his horn

in frustration. But the cars in front of him were hopelessly gridlocked by swarming demonstrators.

Reporters euphemistically referred to the FUTS organization as Foul up the System, even though its leader, Drake Dennis, insisted the initials stood for Fuck up the System. Dennis dubbed himself Commander Doom of the Sunshine Brigade.

"There's Commander Doom," said K.T., pointing.

It was hard to miss him. Well over six feet tall, 280 pounds, with a full black beard and a gleaming shaved head.

"Drake the Fake," Jerry grumped. "The media treat him like some kind of environmental messiah half the time and like a harmless street comedian the other half. He's a damn terrorist, is what he is. Why don't they throw that guy in jail?"

"They repeal the free-speech amendment?" K.T. twitted him. "I must have missed that."

"Free speech? You call what Drake Dennis does free speech? How about the time FUTS set off the smoke bombs outside the Three Mile Island nuclear plant, creating a mushroom cloud and scaring the hell out of half of Pennsylvania? You call that free speech?"

"Yep."

"K.T., you've learned nothing from working for me."

"At least I've got that to be proud of."

Jerry peered through the windshield at Drake Dennis and his followers. The demonstrators apparently were protesting pollution of the Potomac River. They carried banners reading "I Don't Swim in Your Toilet, Don't Shit in My River," and "You Expect Fish to Live in That Crap?" Cameramen zigzagged among the protesters, hefting mini-cams on their shoulders.

"You notice Dennis notified the TV networks?" Jerry sneered. "That's what he wants. Publicity."

Some of the demonstrators were sloshing buckets of brownish glop on the roadway of the bridge.

"That's not really . . . it isn't, is it?" K.T. asked.

"Nah. It's mud or food color. It better be. If they get any of that stuff on my car, I'll get out there and let them feel what it's *really* like to swim in the Potomac."

K.T. put a restraining hand on his arm as if he might really get out of the car and take on the Sunshine Brigade.

As soon as the TV cameramen began packing up their gear, the demonstrators faded away as quickly as they'd come.

Jerry lowered his window, gave the finger to the departing protestors, and resumed the drive to the reception.

CHAPTER FIFTEEN

Jerry was surprised to see a distinctive silver mane towering above the crowd at the cocktail party.

"Look who's here," he said to K.T.

"Who is it?" K.T. breathed into Jerry's chest. She was too short to see.

"Senator Barton Jacobsen, next President of the United States. No doubt accepting kudos for forcing the *Post* to retract its story. I'm going over and congratulate him."

"You would," K.T. said. "I'm going to look for potential guests who have been ducking my phone calls."

Jerry elbowed his way through the throng toward Jacobsen. He was almost overcome by the fumes of perfume and after-shave in the tight-packed crowd. Squeezing by a luscious young woman in basic black, feeling every curve and indentation of her cushiony rump, Jerry finally pushed through to the senator's side.

"Senator! Jerry Knight."

"Hey, Jerry. Good to see you. Love your show. Listen every night."

Jacobsen kept smiling and nodding and shaking hands, moving inexorably through the crowd. Jerry tucked into his wake and moved along with him.

"Glad you nailed those bastards at the *Post*, Senator," he shouted over the noise. "Damn media. Always going after the conservatives."

"They're out of touch with America, Jerry. They were trying to make sure I never sit in the White House. But I refused to let them silence me and my vision for the nation. I am innocent and I was vindicated."

"Why don't you come on the show, Senator?" Jerry proposed. "Tell America what those bastards tried to do to you."

"Might do it, Jerry. Might do it. Talk to Jack VanDyke. Work it out with him. He's here somewhere."

Jerry felt the surge of the crowd pulling him away from Jacobsen. The tide deposited him in a quiet eddy along the fringe.

First he wanted to find a martini and then he wanted to find Jack VanDyke.

He spotted Jacobsen's chief of staff in a corner, his eyes flicking over the scene, taking in everything and everybody.

"Jack? I'm Jerry Knight."

"How you'all doing? Ah listen to your show all the time."

VanDyke's image as an unscrupulous political tough guy was softened by his Southern accent and by his boyish face. He could have passed for the grinning charmer of the freshman class. Or as Huck Finn. Huck Finn with a very dirty mouth.

"You'all the only one in the media tells it like it is. Not like those assholes at the *Post*. You read that shit they printed about the senator? We nailed that cunt, though. Jane Day, little shit. Teach her to fuck with the senator."

"I invited the senator to come on my show and tell how he forced the *Post* to retract its story. He said to check with you on what night he can do it."

It was a gambit Jerry often used to trick underlings of VIP's into thinking that their bosses had agreed to appear on the *Night Talker* show and that only the date remained to be set. But VanDyke was too savvy to fall for it.

"You'all call the office tomorrow, Jerry. Ah'll check our calendar, see if the senator can work it in. He's awful busy these days."

VanDyke never looked at Jerry. His eyes continuously scanned the ballroom, noting who was there, who they were with, who they were talking to.

"Jack, did you know Curtis Davenport?"

"Ah met him a few times. When he testified at the subcommittee. One of them environmental fruitcakes."

"Did you talk to him recently?" Jerry persisted.

"Not recently, no."

Jerry thought VanDyke had paused a half beat before answering. Interviewing people every night in Washington, Jerry had developed a knack for detecting lies. He sensed VanDyke was lying.

"Someone from your office phoned Davenport just before he went on the air the night he was killed."

"That so? And how you'all know that?"

"My producer wrote down the number. I checked it out. It's your office. And she says Davenport returned the call."

"What's the third degree all about, Jerry?" VanDyke's

Southern accent turned mean. "I ain't in the habit of calling fags in the middle of the night."

"Well, somebody at that number called Davenport. And I'm wondering whether the call had something to do with what happened to him."

"What happened to him was some nigger kid beat his head in and stole his wallet." The angrier VanDyke got, the more redneck his vocabulary became.

Jacobsen was nearing the door. VanDyke bolted and they exited together.

Jerry looked around for K.T. He spotted her next to the ransacked crudités platter talking to a veteran House member.

"You didn't invite him to be on the show, did you?" Jerry asked as he guided the producer toward the door. "That gasbag hasn't taken a stand on an issue in thirty years. His finger must be perpetually chapped from wetting it and testing the wind."

"Tell him yourself. He's your guest a week from Friday."

As the escalator deposited Jerry and K.T. in the Marriott's main lobby, an unpleasant-looking man approached them. He was lanky, wearing a nondescript gray suit. His red face, pocked with old acne scars, looked as if it had been rubbed raw with sandpaper.

"Why'd you put that fuck Davenport on your show?" he slurred. Jerry realized he was drunk. "I'm glad somebody killed the fuck. Good riddance. I wish I'd done it myself."

Jerry was too startled to respond. The man staggered onto the escalator and descended toward the ballroom level.

"Who the hell was that?" Jerry asked K.T.

Responsible for recruiting five to ten guests a week for

the *Night Talker* show, the producer was a walking Who's Who.

"I'm almost sure it was Kurt Voss," she replied. "Former congressman. Now he's a lobbyist, cashing in on his contacts."

"And a very ugly drunk," Jerry finished.

CHAPTER SIXTEEN

THE NEXT DAY was Saturday. Since he had no shows on the weekend, Jerry switched to normal hours. He went to bed as soon as the Friday night program concluded and set the alarm for noon. He was sitting in his robe at the wrought-iron table on his balcony, having a lazy brunch of bagels, cream cheese, and coffee, when he read in the *Post* about the memorial service for Curtis Davies Davenport.

It was scheduled for three P.M. at the National Cathedral.

Jerry decided to attend. He wasn't sure why. Maybe it was just a way to fill up an empty Saturday afternoon.

He showered, dressed, and headed his black Cadillac north through Rock Creek Park.

"Get a job like the rest of us!" he yelled through the closed car window to the homeless people slumped beneath the Georgetown bridges.

After that stretch, the route became pastoral.

It was early May and every turn of the twisting parkway presented a new vista of yellow daffodil trumpets and white dogwood blossoms. The narrow green preserve on the banks of Rock Creek ran straight through the heart of Washington. Of the many cities where Jerry had worked, Washington was his favorite. Not the people. The scenery.

He turned off the parkway behind the old Japanese Embassy and drove up the hill. Waiting at the light to turn left onto Massachusetts Avenue, Jerry glanced up at the exotic minaret atop the Islamic Mosque. The mosque was surrounded by taxicabs, their immigrant drivers inside saying their prayers.

Barely a mile up Massachusetts Avenue stood the cathedral, mother church for the city's oldest money and power. Perched on the highest point in Washington, the cathedral was the church where Washington's WASPs were christened, schooled, married, and eulogized.

Davenport's memorial service was being held in the cathedral's main sanctuary, a chamber as large as an airplane hanger. The rich detail of chiseled stone, carved wood, and stained glass was overwhelming, paid for with a hundred years of contributions and bequests from the well-off parishioners.

Building up credits with God, Jerry mused cynically. And the IRS.

The hard, low-backed chairs were bunched together in front of the great stone pulpit. Almost all the seats were taken when Jerry arrived. The people looked small and insignificant under the soaring arches.

While the attendees made their way to their seats, an organ played. In an ornate loft behind the pulpit, rows of men and women in blue robes, seated facing each other, sang softly. Jerry couldn't make out the music. At first he assumed bad acoustics, the vastness of the sanctuary swallowing up the sound. Then he realized the organ and choir were droning through the monotonous mush of New Age music. Davenport's favorite songs, no doubt.

The service had attracted a goodly number of celebrities. Jerry nodded to familiar faces. A couple of senators. The President's press secretary. A cabinet member who was either the secretary of agriculture or secretary of interior, he could never remember which. A lot of environmental activists. Some TV talking heads from the weekend panel shows. Robert Redford representing the Hollywood branch of the green movement.

Several television cameras, shrouded in black cloth, were tucked discreetly against the mammoth stone pillars. So that's why so many VIP's had shown up, Jerry guessed. A chance to be seen at a politically correct event.

The music swelled into the processional. Jerry found a seat next to a woman in a wide-brimmed hat.

A formation of white-robed priests marched in and mounted the pulpit, attended by their acolytes. They were followed by the eulogizers, who took seats roped off for them in the front row. They were there to participate in a Washington ritual in which prominent people, who may or may not know the deceased, recall his or her life in lavish and sometimes exaggerated terms. Meanwhile, Davenport's body had been shipped home to Oregon for burial.

The service began.

"I am the resurrection and the life, saith the Lord; he that believeth in me, though he were dead, yet shall he live; and whosoever liveth and believeth in me shall never die," the priest intoned.

"Accept our prayers on behalf of thy servant Curtis."

Readings. More prayers. Hymns from the choir.

Then, one by one, the eulogizers made their way to the pulpit to praise Davenport's life and mourn his death.

Drake Dennis, bombastic as always. Ted Kennedy, looking like a cartoonist's caricature, pacing through the cadenced phrases written for him. Jesse Jackson blaming Davenport's death on a Reagan-Bush antienvironmental mentality of "earnings before earth, profits before planet."

Jerry couldn't help snorting at that. Several people seated near him turned and stared disapprovingly.

The next speaker was a young woman. Her dark hair was pulled back and tied with a black ribbon at the nape of her neck. Her face was a pale oval with two dark hollows hiding her eyes. She wore a mannish pin-striped suit, a cream-colored silk blouse, and a scarf knotted at her throat.

Jerry checked his program. Jennifer Hurst. She was not otherwise identified. Maybe the girlfriend Detective Jones had mentioned. Maybe a sister or cousin.

"How can I sum up the life of Curtis in just a few words?" Jennifer Hurst spoke softly in contrast to the oratorical style of the preceding eulogists.

"He was a person who believed very strongly in right and wrong. He lived his life, both his public life and his private life, in accord with that principle. Curtis was not a hypocrite. Very few of us could live up to Curtis's standards. We all fell short of what he expected of us."

She paused. Someone sneezed and it rang like a shot in the hush.

"Goodbye, Curtis." The voice of Jennifer Hurst was trembling. "We will miss you. I will strive to match your integrity. May others do the same."

The young woman slowly descended the high pulpit and returned to her seat.

Two more eulogies, more hymns from the choir, more prayers.

"May his soul, and the souls of all the departed, through the mercy of God, rest in peace," the priest concluded.

"Amen," the audience responded.

The organ played the recessional. The service was over.

As Jerry walked to his car, he heard someone call his name.

"Jerry Knight? I'm Jane Day from the *Washington Post*," she introduced herself. They had met once at a party. But Jane was sure he wouldn't remember her. She was right.

"Oh, yeah. You're the one did the hatchet job on Barton Jacobsen."

"I wouldn't call it a hatchet job," she responded assertively. "He took a payoff and I reported it. I thought you conservatives were big on law and order."

"When a conservative does it, it's a payoff. When a liberal does it, it's a campaign contribution. That's the attitude I'd expect from the *Post*."

"Please, Mr. Knight. I don't need any journalism lessons from you."

"That's right." Jerry laughed. "You just *got* a journalism lesson. Jacobsen crammed your story right down your throat and the *Post* had to retract it."

"The paper did *not* retract my story!" the reporter shot back. "It published a clarification."

" 'Clarifying' that you couldn't produce any evidence to back up your hatchet job." Jerry laughed again and kept moving toward his car.

Jane Day trotted beside him. Her face had that irritating intensity he saw in most women reporters. And what weird hair, almost orange, and flying all over the place.

"I want to talk to you about Curtis Davenport," she said.

"You going to blame the conservatives for that, too?"

"You were the last person to see him alive."

"Next to the last person," Jerry corrected her. "Unless you think I killed him."

"Next to the last person," Jane acknowledged. "You may not have killed him. But you were incredibly antagonistic toward him on the air."

"You listened? I'm flattered. I thought my show would be too politically incorrect for your taste."

"It is."

Jerry was at his car. He unlocked the door.

"So I was antagonistic toward Davenport. I'm antagonistic toward all my guests. So what? What's that got to do with his death?"

"I don't know. Nothing, probably. But he was my friend, and now he's dead. I want to know who killed him."

"The cops say it was a street punk who needed money for a drug fix. Maybe if your newspaper stopped coddling criminals, they'd be in jail where they belong and not out on the streets killing your friends."

"You're a creep," Jane hissed. "You make Rush Limbaugh look good."

"And you have a nice day, too."

Jerry got into his Cadillac, slammed the door, and drove off laughing. Any day he could piss off a *Washington Post* reporter was a day well spent.

CHAPTER SEVENTEEN

GERMAINE'S VIETNAMESE-CHINESE restaurant was a half mile south of the cathedral in what real estate agents and merchants liked to call Upper Georgetown. But it was an ordinary traffic-clogged, slightly seedy area of rock 'n' roll taverns, fast-food joints, and an all-night Amoco station, nothing like the real Georgetown a few blocks farther south.

Jane Day climbed the steep flight of stairs to the second-floor restaurant, a favorite hangout of Washington journalists and politicians. A hand-lettered sign, FRIENDS OF CURTIS, was taped to the door. For Curtis's wake, Germaine had closed off the back room. They were already drinking when Jane entered.

The owner, a handsome Vietnamese woman in the traditional *ao di* split skirt and trousers, greeted Jane with a hug.

Jane ordered a white wine and studied the buffet. She zeroed in on a plate piled high with grilled chunks of chicken slathered with peanut sauce and skewered on bamboo slivers. She was on her second skewer, mentally calculating the calories, when she spotted Jennifer Hurst standing alone studying a haunting photo of a weeping Vietnamese child.

Jane knew that Jennifer worked on the Hill and had once been Curtis's girlfriend. Her eulogy had struck Jane as troublingly enigmatic, hinting at something left unsaid. The reporter worked her way across the room to offer her condolences.

"I'm Jane Day. I knew Curtis through his work. I'm so sorry about your loss."

"I remember meeting you," Jennifer said in a weary monotone. Her skin was pale. She had large dark eyes and black hair.

"You wrote the piece in the *Post* about Jacobsen, didn't you?"

"Yes."

"I'm on the staff of his subcommittee. If you had talked to me before you wrote your story, you could have added fanny-pinching to the charges against him."

"They just don't get it, do they?" Jane commiserated. "There's a couple of senators I won't interview unless someone else is in the room."

Jennifer, lost in grief, turned back to the photograph of the sad child.

"Well, I just wanted to tell you how sorry I am about Curtis," Jane said and started to back away.

"Sorry?" Jennifer said quietly. "Your story may have gotten Curtis killed. Do you know that?"

The words stung Jane like a slap across her face.

"What do you mean?" she stammered.

"I know Curtis was your source. And if I know, others know. Maybe somebody didn't like him talking to the newspaper about their campaign contribution and the influence it bought them. Jacobsen has powerful friends. His henchman, VanDyke, is like a Mafia hitman."

"I—I don't . . ." Jane stuttered. "People leak stories every day, bigger stories than this, and they aren't murdered."

"But Curtis was." Jennifer spoke so softly that Jane could barely hear her above the hubbub of the wake. Jennifer stared at Jane, her eyes flat and dead. Then she slowly walked away.

A stress headache started pounding behind Jane's right eye. She'd never considered that Curtis's leak might have offended someone enough to kill him in retaliation. She tried to deny the possibility. But the idea had been planted and it wouldn't go away.

The wake had turned into the typical Washington party. Jane overheard snatches of conversations about real estate, legislation, and the likelihood of the Orioles winning the pennant. Mourners talked about summer beach rentals, an anchorman's nasty divorce, and a congressman's success at inserting pork into a tax bill.

Curtis would have hated the wake, Jane thought. He would have wanted thoughtful discussions of environmental policies, and of what companies should be doing to save the planet.

Jane was thinking about leaving when Jennifer Hurst reappeared. She seemed like a different person. Her voice was loud and she was grinning. Her eyes glistened. She kept rubbing her finger back and forth under her nose.

"I'm sorry, hon," Jennifer apologized with a loud, throaty laugh. "I didn't mean to come down so hard on you. I'm just wrecked by Curtis's death. I don't know what I'm saying."

Jennifer dug in her handbag and came out with a business card.

"Here, call me. We'll get together and talk. You know, we'll talk about . . . we'll talk about everything . . ."

She waded into the crowd and disappeared.

Jane pondered the transformation of Jennifer Hurst. One minute, almost comatose with grief. The next minute babbling with energy. The signs of a cocaine high. She must have gone into the bathroom and snorted. Well, Jane thought, who could blame her under the circumstances?

CHAPTER EIGHTEEN

J<small>ANE NEEDED A</small> drink.

There was a jam-up around the bar at the back, so she left the wake and went to the narrow bar in the front of Germaine's. A large window overlooked Wisconsin Avenue and the softball field across the street. It was the diamond of choice for the city's gay teams. And, some said, occasionally the scene of games played in the nude.

It was early for Saturday diners and drinkers, so the bar was empty except for the bartender. The badge pinned to his tuxedo shirt said he was Michael.

"What are you drinking?" he asked in a tenor voice.

Great voice, Jane thought. And great chest. A nice ruddy Irish face, too.

She ordered white wine. He lifted an open bottle from its bed of ice and poured.

"You here from the wake?" he asked.

Jane nodded.

"I was a friend of Curtis's," the bartender volunteered after she'd taken her first sip. "Sort of a friend. When I heard Germaine was organizing a wake, I offered to help."

"What do you do?" Jane asked. "When you're not bartending at friend's wakes?"

"My real job is also tending bar." Michael smiled. "At Bull Feathers on the Hill. And I'm working on my master's degree at GW. In public administration."

Jane wanted to keep the conversation going. Michael was the most attractive man she'd encountered in a long time.

"Do you believe what the police say about Curtis's murder?" Jane asked. "That it was a random street crime?"

"Are you a cop?"

"No."

"What then?"

"A friend of Curtis's. And a reporter."

"A reporter? Then I'm not talking."

"Why?"

"Because reporters never get it right. They always twist around what you say and make your words come out different from what you intended."

"I won't. I promise," Jane said. He sounded like he knew something. "I was a friend of Curtis's. I'm just trying to find out who killed him."

"Just trying to get a story," Michael corrected her. "Sorry."

She opened her mouth to begin her standard spiel on the indispensable role of a free press in a democratic society. But she couldn't work up the emotional stamina for it tonight.

"Call me if you change your mind," Jane said. She dropped her card on the bar and left.

The crowd at the wake in the back had started to thin out. The buffet table had been picked clean. Jennifer Hurst was still surrounded by a small circle of mourners. Germaine looked as if she wished they would all go home so she could ready the back room for paying customers.

Jane decided to leave without saying goodbye.

CHAPTER NINETEEN

OUT ON WISCONSIN Avenue, the Saturday-night crowd was growing. A lot of Georgetown University students. A lot of Georgetown University wannabes from lesser schools. High schoolers from the suburbs hoping to pass for college students.

Jane stood on the sidewalk uncertainly. She had nothing to do. No date. No movie she was dying to see or book she couldn't wait to get back to. Each hand-in-hand couple, each laughing group, deepened her sense of loneliness.

Michael was a hunk. But forget that.

She could go back to her apartment, of course. Rot her brain on idiotic sitcoms. Play with Bloomsbury. But he would be sleeping. Or disdainful. She wished she could be as self-sufficient as her cat.

She decided to go to the office.

A cab was just unloading a group headed for Germaine's. Jane got in and gave the familiar Fifteenth Street address.

"Where the hell have you been?" Bill Upshaw greeted her brusquely. "I've been trying to find you."

"Why?"

"Helmsley was supposed to cover the Davenport memorial service," the Saturday editor explained. "But she got pulled off to cover a shooting in Cleveland Park. Kid cutting the grass in front of his house was killed by some crazy guy out on parole. Somebody told me you were at the memorial service. I need you to write a piece. We used the wires in the early edition. But I need a byline piece for the home edition. Five hundred words. Fast."

Jane went to her cubicle and turned on her computer. The newsroom was quiet and mostly empty. Only a few news assistants making their calls to police departments and fire departments. A few editors keeping an eye on the wires, talking on the phone to reporters in places where it was already Sunday morning, and poring over early editions of the *New York Times* to make sure the great rival didn't have a story the *Post* had missed.

Jane felt at home in the newsroom when it was like this. It enveloped her like a comforter. She walked to the coffee room and returned with a hot cup, secure on this familiar turf.

Before beginning her own story, she scrolled through the wire services on her screen, reading what their reporters had written about the memorial service.

The AP played it like a political story, saying the service was attended by "a who's who of government and environmental leaders." Kennedy and Jackson were quoted.

Reuters took an approach more likely to appeal to its

predominantly European audience: "Washington, D.C.'s infamous murder rate was brought home to its power elite Saturday as hundreds of mourners turned out to pay tribute to the latest victim of street gangs . . ."

Within an hour, Jane had written her account, part tribute, part anecdote-filled feature story, part straight reporting.

She read through the skimpy notes from her abbreviated interview with Jerry Knight and considered whether to include them. She decided not to. Not enough there. Knight was such a creep. But in a town of temporizers, at least he stuck by his beliefs.

She keyed her story over to Edit. It was in Upshaw's hands now.

She was about to log off when the phone rang.

Odd. Nobody knew she was in the newsroom on Saturday night.

"Jane Day."

"Hi. This is Michael. The bartender? From Germaine's?"

Jane pumped her fist into the air. After such a long dry spell, could this attractive man actually be interested in her? Or was he interested in telling her what he knew about Curtis? She wasn't sure which she would prefer.

"I thought you don't talk to reporters."

"I don't, usually. But I've been thinking about what you said. About wanting to find out who killed Curtis. You sounded like you meant it."

"I did!" Jane blurted out overenthusiastically. "You know something that will help?"

"Maybe. It could be connected to his death. Or maybe it's nothing. But it's been bothering me ever since he was killed."

"What is it?"

Jane's hands were poised over her keyboard, ready to make notes.

"Not over the phone," Michael said. "I'm tending bar tonight at Bull Feathers. You know it? On the Hill? I get a fifteen-minute break at eight forty-five. Come to the bar and we'll talk."

"I'll be there."

CHAPTER TWENTY

$\mathcal{S}$HE SPOTTED MICHAEL before he saw her. He was reaching down for something below the bar. She'd been right about the chest. He had slicked back his blond hair for Saturday-night duty.

Bull Feathers was on the ground floor of a square brick building four blocks south of the Capitol. It stood on the borderline between the relatively safe environs of the congressional offices, and the unpredictable, ungentrified surrounding neighborhood.

The place tried hard to evoke the atmosphere of a British pub. Dark-wood-and-frosted-glass dividers. Fake Tiffany chandeliers. Gold velour cafe curtains on thick round rods in the front windows. But the two TV sets showing baseball in the back and the rows of modern recessed cone lights in the low composite-board ceiling ruined the effect.

Bull Feathers was more a neighborhood hamburger

joint with pretensions than a pub. It attracted a mixed crowd of congressional interns and receptionists, senior staffers and lobbyists, and occasionally an actual Member.

Jane slid onto a stool at the long white marble bar.

Michael noticed her immediately. His ruddy, freckled face crinkled into a broad smile.

"Want a drink while you're waiting?" he asked. "On the house."

Jane shook her head. She munched peanuts and surveyed the menu while she waited for Michael's break.

Burger Burgers, Classic Burgers, Bull Burgers, Capitol Hill Burgers, and Turkey Burgers. Bull Feathers was known for its burgers. In fact, the menu proclaimed that its burgers had been voted Capitol Hill's best.

The bar was not crowded. Happy hour was long past. The waiting dinner customers had all been seated and the after-movie drinkers had not yet arrived.

She stared at Michael's chest as he lifted his apron over his head. He grabbed a half-empty bottle of Chardonnay and two glasses and motioned her to follow him to the kitchen in the back, behind the TV sets.

The sizzle of fat sang on the grills. Waiters shouted orders. Chefs cursed and flung food onto plates.

Michael led Jane to a quiet alcove off the kitchen, away from the chaos but still within range of the aromas. A round table and six chairs were set up for employees.

Michael poured wine into the two glasses, raised his in a wordless toast, and drank. She did the same.

"I've got to be back in fifteen minutes," he began. He looked troubled. "I'm still not sure I should be talking to a reporter."

"I'm a friend of Curtis's first and a reporter second," Jane replied, trying to reassure him. "You said on the phone you believed me when I said I want to find out who killed him."

"Well, still . . ." He looked at her, took another swallow of his wine, looked at her some more.

"If you know who killed Curtis or why he was killed, you should tell me," Jane prompted.

"I don't want my name used in the newspaper." He seemed to have made up his mind. "Off the record. Okay?"

"Off the record."

"My name won't be printed?"

"I promise."

Jane decided not to pull out her notebook. It might spook him. She'd remember what he said and write it down as soon as she got outside.

"Curtis and Jennifer came in here a lot," Michael began. "A couple of nights a week. Always drank Sam Adams."

Jane nodded and said nothing.

"I got to know them pretty well at the bar. We talked a lot, about Curtis's work, stuff Jennifer was into on the Hill. And a lot of times I'd overhear them talking . . . Off the record, right?"

"Off the record," Jane promised him again.

"I knew Jennifer was stuffing a lot of coke up her nose. I knew Curtis didn't like it. And I was here the night they broke up."

Jane desperately wanted to make notes, but she was afraid of frightening Michael into silence.

"They broke up because of the coke?" Jane guessed.

Michael nodded.

That confirmed her suspicions about Jennifer's sudden transformation at Germaine's.

"They were sitting at the front two bar stools the night he told her he'd had enough of her coke habit. I don't know what she said to set him off, but he lost his temper completely, loud enough for the whole place to hear him."

"What did he say to her?"

"Curtis said if she didn't kick her habit, he was going to expose the 'whole thing' or the 'whole ring.' I'm not sure which he said. But he said it loud. A lot of people heard him."

"You think somebody overheard the threat, somebody selling drugs maybe, and killed him to keep him from blowing the whistle on the 'ring'?"

"I think it's possible," Michael said. He looked at his watch.

"I've got to go back on duty." He gulped down the rest of his wine and stood up.

"Will you tell this to the cops?" Jane asked.

"Are you out of your mind? No way! The drug dealers know who talks to the cops. I can't afford that kind of trouble. I've got a family to feed."

What? Jane looked at his left hand. No ring. There ought to be a law requiring married men to wear a ring!

"I'll deny I ever talked to you if this gets traced to me," he said.

"I told you I'd protect you," she assured him again, sneaking one last look at his chest. "Your name will never appear."

"Good. And good luck."

He reached out to shake her hand. She took it, squeezed slightly, and let it go. Reluctantly.

"Be careful," he warned in his vibrant tenor.

When Michael had returned to duty at the bar, Jane rushed to the ladies' room just outside the kitchen and wrote down everything she could remember in her notebook.

CHAPTER TWENTY-ONE

SUNDAY CAME TOO soon.

Returning to her empty apartment Saturday night after the meeting with Michael, Jane had flopped onto the couch and skimmed the cable channels, finally stopping at a black-and-white forties movie starring Deborah Kerr and some guy whose name she couldn't remember. She finished off a bag of butter-free popcorn and a half bottle of slightly vinegary white wine. She awakened at three-thirty A.M., the TV still on, now showing a World War II movie. She crawled into bed, still wearing her underwear. Sunday she could sleep late.

Bloomsbury had other ideas. At seven A.M. he hopped onto the bed, strode across the blankets, and tickled her awake with his whiskers. Breakfast time! Jane groaned. The cat curled up on her chest, purring loudly. He knew she couldn't resist him, and before long she'd be out of bed, running a can of tuna through the electric opener. His favorite sound.

After feeding Bloomsbury, Jane made a pot of extra-strength French Roast, dragged the Sunday paper in from the hallway, and returned to bed.

Her account of the Davenport memorial service was on page A7. Not bad placement. And not a bad piece, considering she had written it under the gun after two glasses of wine.

Jane got up, retrieved her notebook from her shoulder bag, and returned to bed to review her notes from the conversation with Michael.

Ah, Michael.

Forget it!

She knew the paper would never run a story based on one conversation with a bartender who wouldn't let his name be printed. Especially after what happened with her Jacobsen story.

She needed a second source, and there was only one other source. Jennifer Hurst. Jennifer had given her a business card and said call. Jane retrieved the card from her purse. Office number only. No home phone.

Jane pulled the phone book from the top shelf of her overcrowded closet. Jennifer was single, working on the Hill, so Jane assumed she lived in the city.

There was a J. Hurst listed on P Street NW and a J. R. Hurst on East Capitol Street. She tried J. A scratchy recording of a man's voice answered. Jane hung up. She punched in the number for J. R. A woman answered on the third ring, sounding hung over. Jane recognized Jennifer's voice. She hung up without speaking.

Jane was sure Jennifer would never talk over the phone

about the scene in Bull Feathers. And she probably wouldn't agree to a meeting if she knew what Jane wanted to talk about. Jane's only hope of confirming the story was to show up unannounced on Jennifer's doorstep.

The cab driver did not speak or understand English. So after a roundabout ride, Jane gave up, paid him, got out in front of the Supreme Court building, and walked the last few blocks.

Jennifer Hurst lived in an apartment building four blocks east of the Capitol, close to the Library of Congress. The five-story building, with its large lush lawn, stood out on a street of low, old town houses.

The building dated from the nineteenth century but was well maintained, its stone facade painted a creamy color with black and gray trim. An ornate cornice decorated the top.

Jane climbed the redbrick steps to the entrance. A bas relief of an American eagle stretched across the top of the front door. She checked the mailboxes. Jennifer lived on the top floor in front.

After a long wait, Jennifer answered Jane's knock. She looked surprised. She also looked awful. Without makeup, her skin was sallow. The wrinkles around her eyes were pronounced. She wore blue jeans and a gray sweatshirt. She was barefoot.

"I'm sorry to bother you at home, Jennifer." Jane rushed the words, trying to talk her way in before Jennifer could close the door on her. "I have something very important I need to talk to you about."

Jennifer stared at Jane. Her eyes were flat, the way they'd been before her transformation at Germaine's. Jane noticed that there was a lot of gray in her black hair.

"Come in," Jennifer said after a long pause.

She led Jane to a flowered love seat in a sunny bay window overlooking East Capitol Street. Jane could see the white dome of the Capitol building at the end of the street.

Jennifer brought a silver tray holding two plain white china cups and saucers, a white china coffeepot, cream, sugar, and two small silver spoons.

She seated herself in an identical love seat opposite Jane.

"You want to talk to me about something 'very important.'" It was half statement, half question.

"Jennifer, this is very difficult for me," Jane began haltingly. She'd tried to formulate her pitch in the cab. But nothing had sounded right. She'd have to make it up as she went along.

"It's about Curtis?" Jennifer prompted.

"Yes."

"And me?"

"Yes."

Jennifer stirred cream into her coffee. Jane extracted her notebook from her tapestry bag.

"Someone told me you and Curtis had an argument in . . . in a restaurant. And—"

"And Curtis threatened to stop seeing me and to turn in my dealer if I didn't stop using coke," Jennifer finished. "Is that what you heard?"

"Yes."

"It doesn't surprise me. Curtis was very angry. The place was full of people. Bull Feathers. A lot of people must have heard him."

Jane sipped her coffee. Jennifer sipped her coffee. The sound of a siren penetrated the cozy bay window.

"You want to print this in your newspaper?"

"Yes."

"Why?"

"Maybe somebody in the bar heard what Curtis said and felt threatened by it. Maybe somebody in the drug business on Capitol Hill—"

"There are plenty of them," Jennifer interrupted bitterly.

"Maybe whoever heard him decided to kill him to stop him from exposing their drug business."

"Why do you want to put this in your paper? Curtis is dead." Jennifer lifted her cup with a shaking hand. "Even if that's why he was killed, what good would it do? It's too late."

"The police are dismissing his murder as random street violence." This part Jane had worked out in the cab. "They're not seriously looking for his murderer. A story in the *Post* suggesting that drug dealers had killed him to stop him from exposing their business on the Hill would force the police to launch a serious investigation."

"I see."

Jennifer poured more coffee, stirred in more cream.

"It's the way in Washington, isn't it?" she mused, almost to herself. "The power of the press. You want something done, you've got to attract the attention of the media first."

They were both silent for a while.

"I would be destroyed," Jennifer said in a very low voice. "I've worked ten years on the Hill. It hasn't been easy, for a woman. But I've hung in there. I've advanced. And if you write this, I'm destroyed."

"In your eulogy yesterday, you said you would strive to live up to Curtis's standards of integrity," Jane recalled. "Don't you think he'd want the drug dealers caught, no matter what the price?"

"You're good," Jennifer said caustically. "You think you know just which buttons to push."

She paused.

"Can you write it without using my name?"

Jane was careful not to show her elation. Jennifer had as much as agreed. She was just bargaining over terms now.

"I might be able to write the story without using your name. But I'll have to tell my editors, privately."

"Tell your editors . . . ?"

"So they can be sure I got the story from a reliable source. But we wouldn't have to print your name."

"The police will certainly want to know the name of your source. These days, witnesses . . . I mean, there's a danger . . ."

"We *never* tell the police our sources," Jane said reassuringly.

Jennifer got up from the love seat and paced. She seemed agitated.

"Curtis . . ." Jennifer sighed.

"Curtis would want you to do the right thing." Jane held her breath.

Jennifer paced to the hallway and back again. And then again. Jane was afraid she might disappear and return on a coke high.

"All right."

Jennifer said it so softly Jane wasn't sure she'd heard it.

"It's all right?" she asked, for confirmation.

"Please. Please don't print my name."

"I promise."

Jennifer moved toward the front door. Their meeting was over. Jane put her notebook away, rose, and followed her to the door.

"Jennifer?"

"Hmmm?"

"Can you quit?"

"I'm trying. I'm trying but it's so hard."

She closed the door behind Jane.

Jane guessed Jennifer would be sniffing white powder before she could find a cab.

CHAPTER TWENTY-TWO

J ANE WENT STRAIGHT to the *Post* from Jennifer's apartment.

Russ Williamson was on duty. This was good because she didn't have to deal with an unfamiliar Sunday editor. It was bad, however, because he was still angry at her for burning him on the Jacobsen story.

She told him what she'd learned from Michael and Jennifer, leaving out the names. She argued that the incident at Bull Feathers justified a story. Curtis Davenport had been overheard threatening to expose a Capitol Hill drug ring, and might have been killed by the dealers to silence him.

"Oh no, not again!" Russ moaned. "Everybody wants to be an investigative reporter these days. Doesn't anyone just cover news conferences anymore? Whatever happened to accurate quotes with full attribution?"

Russ wasn't about to risk his neck again. He phoned Kirk Scoffield at his weekend home in Middleburg, Virginia, interrupting a lawn party the executive editor and his wife, a TV anchorwoman, were giving for a retiring columnist.

Russ put Jane on an extension. Scoffield made her repeat her story over and over again, asking questions, poking holes, pressing for more details. Finally, Scoffield demanded to know the names of her sources.

"I promised we wouldn't print their names," Jane protested.

"Goddamn it," Scoffield exploded. "I don't give a shit what you promised. I want to know who the hell your sources are. You got my ass in a crack once, and once is once too often. I'm not going to run away from a good story, but I'm sure as hell not going to let you send me and this newspaper down the tubes twice! You tell me who the hell your sources are, kid, or this conversation is over."

And my career, too, Jane guessed.

She told Scoffield about her meetings with Michael and Jennifer. He quieted down.

After another twenty minutes of haggling, Scoffield agreed to run the story, but under a conservative headline, inside the Metro section, heavily qualified with a lot of "mights" and "coulds" and "may haves." And with police reaction.

The editor ordered Russ to call him back and read him the finished story for final approval.

Chastened, Jane retreated to her computer and wrote the story in accordance with Scoffield's instructions.

She phoned Homicide and asked for the detective in charge of the Davenport investigation. He was out on another case. She left her name and number. He didn't call back by deadline time. She added a line to her story saying that the police had no comment.

CHAPTER TWENTY-THREE

W HAT'S THIS CRAP in the *Post*?"

A. L. Jones stood in front of Captain Wheeler's desk. He didn't know which crap in the *Post* his superior was referring to. And the captain was waving the paper so wildly, the detective couldn't read it.

"MURDERED ENVIRONMENTALIST THREATENED HILL DRUG EXPOSURE." Wheeler read the headline aloud.

Jones hadn't had time to read the morning paper. He'd been up all night trying to find out who had shot into a pickup basketball game on a blacktop court on Livingston Road, killing two of the players.

He wished he hadn't left his cup of coffee on his desk when the captain had summoned him. Jones felt fuzzy-headed. He tried hard to concentrate.

"You know anything about this?" the captain demanded, throwing the newspaper across the desk.

Jones studied the article. It was about Davenport, the

white guy beaten to death in the parking garage on M Street. Seems he had announced in a bar one night that he was going to expose drug-dealing on the Hill if his girlfriend didn't stop snorting coke.

"No sir, I don't know anything about it," A.L. confessed. "First I heard of it."

The captain stood up and stared through the dirty window behind his desk.

"A.L., I'm getting heat on this case. The mayor called. Jesse Jackson called. White dude, everybody knows him, busted right downtown."

Wheeler was a thin, light-skinned black man with a moustache that looked as if it were drawn on with a pencil. He was dressed in a three-piece tan suit, a little ahead of the season, a starched white shirt, and a narrow purple necktie.

The rumor in Homicide was that Wheeler was tight with the mayor and was on his way to bigger things, maybe chief. He didn't need the unsolved murder of a white guy to screw up his future.

"Mayor's afraid it's going to hurt the tourist business," Wheeler reported. "It was bad enough when it looked like a robbery gone bad. We're really going to see some heat if it was a drug gang busting a white man to shut him up. You got to nail this one, A.L. I mean fast."

"I've got it covered, Captain."

"A.L., you're looking to get out of Homicide, aren't you?"

"I can take it or leave it."

"But you'd just as soon leave it, wouldn't you? Transfer to the Routine Squad? Investigate all those nice simple heart attacks and drownings? No more drive-bys. No more drug boys beefing your witnesses. No more creeping up dark stairwells in the projects at four o'clock in the morning scared shitless."

"You ought to be in recruiting, Captain. You make it sound *so* appealing."

"You bring in the mother who did Davenport, I'll transfer you to the Routine Squad, A.L. Work regular hours. Do wonders for your social life."

"I'd miss them stairwells."

The captain snatched back the paper.

"Listen to this part," Wheeler commanded. " 'Davenport's friend agreed to tell her story to the *Post* on the condition that her name not be disclosed.' What bullshit! Get the name of the friend. Talk to her. Shake your eyes. Find out who her dealer was. You gotta close this one, A.L."

"No sweat."

The detective headed back to his desk. When he got there, his coffee was cold.

CHAPTER TWENTY-FOUR

Naturally, Scoffield zeroed in on the one weak spot in Jane's story.

"I thought I told you to include police reaction!" he exploded as soon as she hit the office Monday morning.

"I called but they never called back," Jane stammered.

"Then you goddamn write that you couldn't reach the police, not that they had no comment. Jesus Christ, you're worse than a goddamn TV reporter."

The ultimate insult.

"Get your ass down to Homicide and get their story," Russ Williamson ordered, loud enough for Scoffield to hear. Covering his backside again, Jane noted.

Jane took a cab to the city's squat, square, ugly Municipal Center on Indiana Avenue. She found the cluttered warren of Homicide offices on the third floor. She looked incredibly out of place in a tailored red plaid suit with gold buttons and matching earrings.

A uniformed policewoman, stationed at a battered metal desk just inside the door appraised her and asked who she was looking for.

"The detective handling the Davenport case."

"And you are?"

"Jane Day. *Washington Post*." She held out a laminated photo ID badge hanging on a chain around her neck.

"I'll see if he's in."

The policewoman shouted into the din, "Hey, A.L. You famous or something, honey? Reporter here to see you. From the *Washington Post*. Better hitch up your tie."

A.L. appeared, tie unhitched.

"I'm Detective Jones," he introduced himself in a deep baritone.

"I'm Jane Day. *Washington Post*."

"Yeah? I just called you at your office."

"Why?"

"Probably the same reason you're here. Come on."

He led her into the commotion of the Homicide offices, through a maze of metal desks, past sullen suspects slumped in their chairs, around a black-and-white TV set blaring *The Price is Right*, and into a tiny windowless room. A round table, scarred with cigarette burns, and two metal folding chairs almost completely filled the space.

"This is where you beat the confessions out?" Jane asked with mock seriousness.

"Yep. This is it," A.L. replied with an equally straight face. "We hide the batons and the rubber hoses when reporters come around. Coffee?"

She hesitated.

"It's bad," he advised.

"I'll skip it."

"Good choice."

She pulled a notebook from her shoulder bag.

"Are you investigating any connection between Curtis Davenport's murder and his threat in the . . . in a bar to expose a Capitol Hill drug ring?" she asked abruptly.

"Whoa. That ain't the way it works here. *I* ask the questions."

"Sorry, Detective Jones. *I'm* a reporter. *I* ask the questions."

"From the newspaper this morning, looks like you know more than I know. So *I'm* asking *you* the questions."

She laughed at that notion.

"Detective, don't be ridiculous."

He slammed his fist down hard on table. She jerked back in surprise.

"Ain't nothing funny, Miss Washington Post," he rumbled. "And ain't nothing ridiculous. Man's dead. I'm trying to find who killed him."

He kicked the door shut. Jane was not accustomed to this kind of treatment. Most of the people she interviewed treated her with excessive deference, hoping to sweet-talk her into writing something favorable about them. Jones wasn't like that at all.

"You know something that might help me catch whoever dropped Davenport," A.L. told her, sticking his face up close to hers. "The girlfriend is Jennifer Hertz, Hurst, something like that, right? And I need to know the bar where they had this argument about her coke habit."

"Detective Jones, I can't reveal my sources," she chanted like a mantra.

He slammed his fist down on the table again.

"Goddamn it, don't give me that crap. This ain't about putting stories in the newspaper. It's about murder."

"Stop yelling at me!" Jane said firmly. "I *know* it's about murder. Curtis was a friend of mine."

"Then help me!"

"I can't tell you anything. I promised I wouldn't."

They sat staring at each other in the tiny dark room.

Irritating bitch, Jones fumed.

"Just 'cause you're a reporter, doesn't make you exempt from being a good citizen," the detective told her. "You've got to live in this city with the rest of us. Don't you *want* to get these creeps off the street?"

"You don't even know if the scene in the bar had anything to do with Curtis's death," Jane replied. "You've been saying it was a random street crime."

"At least let me check it out."

"I can't violate my promise. If reporters don't live up to their promises of confidentiality, pretty soon no one will trust us."

"Hell!" Jones exploded. "Nobody trusts you now!"

"Sorry."

"I don't know how you can look yourself in the mirror," the detective said in disgust.

"I'll make you a deal," Jane offered. "You let me quote you saying the police are investigating whether the scene in the bar had anything to do with Curtis's murder, and I'll tell you the name of the bar."

"I don't make deals for information," Jones told her.

"I don't usually make deals for information, either," she lied. "Can I quote you that you're investigating?" she pressed.

"Don't use my name. Just say the police are investigating."

"I'm going to say 'a police source says.' "

" 'A police source'? Okay. But not my name. What's the bar?"

"Bull Feathers."

"And the girl is Jennifer, right."

"I'm not going to confirm that."

"You ain't denying it either."

A. L. Jones stood up abruptly, yanked open the door, and stalked out.

"Nice doing business with you, Miss Washington Post."

She didn't like him. But she had her piece for tomorrow: "Responding to a story that first appeared in the *Washington Post*, D.C. police are trying to determine whether a threat by environmentalist Curtis Davenport to expose a Capitol Hill drug ring was connected with his murder."

CHAPTER TWENTY-FIVE

A. L. JONES STEERED his vanilla white Ford across the South Capitol Street Bridge into the neighborhood he called the badass part of town.

Anacostia.

Nearly five hundred people were murdered every year in the nation's capital. Drugs were involved in most of the murders. And Anacostia was the bloodiest of the killing fields on which Washington's drug wars were fought.

Jones turned right off the deceptively scenic Suitland Parkway onto Alabama Avenue. He drove past block after block of dilapidated houses and depressing low-income government apartment buildings. Two-story redbrick structures, ironically called garden apartments, devoid of distinctiveness except for swirls of spray-paint graffiti. Windows boarded up. Doors ripped off their hinges.

Abandoned cars rusted in the trash-strewn streets,

wheels gone, hoods and trunks gaping, everything worth stealing ripped out.

Elsewhere at this season, Washington was abloom with jonquils and tulips, forsythia and new grass. Here the landscape was dirt and dead gray trees.

The people were as alien as the setting. Motionless, doing nothing, sitting on front stoops or curbs, leaning against trees, congregated in furtive groups. They silently tracked Jones with their eyes.

The only sign of activity was a basketball game on a school playground.

Menace hung in the air like a stink. The odor of impending violence, of something bad about to happen. Even A.L., a cop with a badge and a gun and a radio, felt the threat.

Jones pulled his car to a stop next to a vacant lot littered with paper, cans, bottles, mattresses, and broken furniture.

Jones switched off his engine, rolled down the window, and waited.

There but for the grace, he thought. He'd grown up in Washington, in neighborhoods almost this bad. He'd hung with a bad crowd. A lot of boys he'd hung with were dead. Including his brother, gunned down holding up a liquor store. A lot of Jones's boyhood friends were crazy from drugs. A lot were in prison. How come he went a different way? Luck. His mother and father. Determination, from God knows where, to make something of himself.

Lately he wondered whether it made any difference what he'd decided to do with his life. People like him were losing ground.

A black kid about twelve years old appeared beside the car.

"What you want, man?"

"Want to talk to Frog."

"Who?"

"Don't give me that jive shit. You know who Frog is and you know who I am."

The boy stared at Jones insolently. Jones stared back.

"Come on," the boy said after a moment.

The detective got out of the car and locked the door. He followed the boy, who walked with a rolling swagger. The young man was dressed in a gray Hoyas Basketball T-shirt, baggy black shorts, and an elaborate pair of Nike high-top sneakers. A beeper was hooked to the waistband of his shorts.

"How come you ain't in school?"

"Mama say I don't got to be in no school."

"You tell your mama A.L. says you better be in school next time I come around."

At the corner the boy turned right. After a block, the street ended at the entrance to a cemetery. A rusted arch over the entry bore Hebrew characters.

Anacostia had once been a white working-class neighborhood. Many of the residents had been Jewish shopkeepers, tailors and furriers, bakers, first-generation immigrants from Eastern Europe and Russia. This was their cemetery.

Then, blacks had begun to crowd into Anacostia, looking for inexpensive places to live after white professionals had taken over and renovated their rundown neighborhoods in Georgetown, Capitol Hill, and Southwest.

The boy led Jones through the tight-packed tombstones carved with Stars of David. At the far end of the cemetery were three black men, leaning against a sooty monument to MYRON GOLDFARB, BELOVED HUSBAND AND FATHER, 1882–1942.

Two of the men were teenagers. One wore an X baseball cap. The other had his cap turned backward. Beneath their T-shirts, they both sported conspicuous bulges that the detective assumed were guns.

The third man was older, in his twenties, wearing a stylish green suit in the baggy Italian style, a black silk shirt unbuttoned halfway down his chest, and lots of gold. A gold earring, gold chains showing through his open shirt, several gold rings, and a heavy gold watch.

It was a local gang, known as the Cemetery Crew.

"Hey, Frog," Jones greeted the one in the suit. "How you doing, man."

The nickname was appropriate. The man's head was squashed, his eyes protruded. He did, indeed, look like a frog.

"What you lookin' for around here, man, your mama?"

Frog's three cronies grinned appreciatively.

"My mama hang with trash like you, she whip your black ass and send you to bed without your supper."

"Hey, man, what's your problem?" Frog snarled. "What you want?"

"Information."

"Why don't you be watching TV? They got a lot of information on there."

The three acolytes laughed at that one.

"Don't be dissin' me, man. I run your ass in quick as shit."

Frog didn't reply.

"Who's selling coke at the Capitol?" Jones demanded.

"Who ain't."

Jones looked hard at the three sidekicks as they tried to suppress their grins.

"I asked you who's dealing at the Capitol," the detective pressed.

"What I get out of it I tell you something?"

"What you get out of it is I don't send your ass to Lorton."

"Lorton!" Frog's squashed face took on an exaggerated look of innocence at Jones's threat to send him to Washington's prison in the Virginia countryside. "For what?"

"Don't mess with me, motherfucker." Jones's tone turned hard. "That brother they found busted in the dumpster out behind McDonald's on Benning Road owed you some serious money, I hear. Maybe I take you in, ask you some questions about that."

"Oh, man!"

"Oh, man!" Jones mimicked.

Nobody said anything for a moment. Suddenly, off to the right, four sharp cracks sounded. Drug boys shooting at each other, Jones guessed. But there was no reaction from the participants in the little tableau in the cemetery, except the two teenagers edged their hands closer to the bulges under their T-shirts.

"What kind of coke you interested in?" Frog asked. "Rock or powder?"

"Powder."

"Yeah? Ain't too many dudes be dealing powder no more."

"Name one."

Frog didn't respond. Jones understood his reluctance. In the drug wars, informers were regularly marked for death. The victims in many of Washington's murders were people who had fingered bandits for the police. But Jones didn't give a shit if he put Frog in danger. Save the city the cost of a trial.

"The brother in the dumpster?" Jones prompted. "Owed you the money?"

"Let me think." Frog squinched up his features in a parody of searching his memory. "I do recollect one person might sell a little powder up there on the Hill."

"Name?"

"Don't know no name. She be some fine white bitch."

The three colleagues murmured agreement.

"Customer of yours?"

"Maybe."

"And you don't know her name?"

"Hey, man, we don't take no American Express."

One of the teenagers laughed at that.

"How you get the shit to her?"

"Once a week, like every Thursday, she park her car at the train station, like on the top level, you know? She get herself something to eat in one of them restaurants in the station, called Sfuzzi, Sfuzzi's, something like that."

The sound of the name made the crew members grin.

"Sfuuuzzi," one of them sang.

"While she be eating, I drop the shit on the back floor of her car," Frog explained. "And I take the money she leave."

"How much?"

"Oh, man!"

"How much?" Jones pressed.

"Half key."

"And you don't know no name?"

"I said I don't, didn't I?"

"How about the car?"

"Silver beemer. Rag top. Man, that be a fine machine."

"You remember the license tag number?"

"I might."

"Yeah?"

"Yeah. I might remember if you forget the brother in the dumpster."

"You ain't got no bargaining power, motherfucker! What's the goddamn license number?"

"It ain't no number, man. It's letters."

"Yeah? What letters?"

"H-O-W-L."

"H-O-W-L?"

"Yeah, like 'howl.' " Frog tilted his squashed head back and howled at the sky like a wolf. His three assistants laughed and nudged each other.

"I didn't know you could spell, Frog," Jones said. "Maybe them schools ain't so bad after all. You sure them's the letters?"

"Yeah, I'm sure, man. How'm I gonna forget something like 'howl'?" He tipped his head back and howled again.

"I don't remember nothin' about no dumpster," Jones told him. "Next week, maybe I remember something."

"You asshole! Get the fuck out of my face, man! Get the fuck out!"

Frog had to show his crew he wasn't intimidated by the cop.

"Don't bother showing me out," Jones said. "I can find the way."

The detective walked away, through the tombstones, tense, itching between the shoulder blades, half expecting one of the drug boys to shoot him in the back.

As A.L. was about to get into his car, an ancient black woman sitting on the steps of a decrepit wooden house across the street motioned to him. He went to her.

"You Detective Jones, ain't ya?" She was dressed in a dusty, shapeless pink housedress.

"Yes, ma'am, I am."

He remembered her. Her grandson had been gunned down five years ago as he stepped out of Frederick Douglass Junior High School. Jones had broken the news to her.

She put her lips up close to his ear.

"One of them boys hanging with Frog, the tall one? He be the one shot that girl in the cleaners on Naylor Road."

"Yeah? You sure?"

"Sure I'm sure," she said in a wispy voice. "But don't tell nobody I told you."

He wouldn't. If the Cemetery Crew knew she'd talked to him, she'd be dead by morning. Why'd she take the risk? Old-fashioned, probably. Still thought people ought to help the cops catch the criminals.

"Thank you," Jones said.

"You get 'em, now, you hear?"

"I will."

She reminded him of his grandmother in North Carolina. Long dead. His family had shipped him and his brother there for the summers when they were growing up. How far away and long ago that peaceful rural place seemed now.

As soon as the detective was back in his car, he radioed the office to check the license tag.

As he was crossing back over the South Capitol Street Bridge, a scratchy voice came on the radio.

"A.L., that tag? Registered to a Patricia Howell. Hotel-Oscar-Whiskey-Echo-Lima-Lima. White female. Forty-two years old. Georgetown address. You want more?"

"Yeah. Give me that address."

CHAPTER TWENTY-SIX

Patricia Howell lived on R Street, facing Montrose Park, on the northern edge of Georgetown. It was the only part of Georgetown where parking spaces could readily be found at the curb, even at seven-thirty P.M., when the residents were returning home from work. So A. L. Jones was able to park just half a block from the address radioed to him.

Her home was one in a row of narrow three-story red-brick town houses. Bay windows jutted out from the upper floors like turrets. The houses stood close to the sidewalk, behind tiny grass plots no bigger than a kitchen table. The ground-floor windows were protected with vertical black iron bars.

Most of the front doors were painted shiny black. A few nonconformists had painted their doors maroon or dark green. How'd the Fine Arts Commission let them get away with that? Jones wondered. Ever since his abbreviated architecture courses at Howard, Jones had noticed details like that as he traveled around Washington.

The detective climbed the two black wrought-iron steps at the Howell address. On either side of the front door was a shiny brass and glass lantern, meant to look like gas lamps from Georgetown's earlier days. Actually, they were illuminated by light bulbs.

Jones pressed the doorbell. From inside, he heard a chime, and in a moment, he heard someone descending a stairway. The white curtain covering a pane of wavy old glass in the door was pulled aside slightly, revealing a woman's face. The curtain was quickly dropped back into place.

"What do you want?" a woman's voice called from inside.

"I'm Detective A. L. Jones of the Metropolitan Police Department. I need to talk to Patricia Howell."

There was no immediate response. Then, the sound of a deadbolt lock being turned. The shiny black door opened an inch, restrained by a gold-colored chain. A woman's eye—plucked brow, heavy eye shadow, curled and blackened lashes—and a slice of her face appeared in the opening.

"Do you have any ID?" the woman demanded.

A slightly disheveled black man appearing on a doorstep as darkness fell in mostly white, mostly rich, robbery-phobic Georgetown aroused a certain suspicion.

A.L. opened the black leather folder containing his badge and photo ID and held it up to the narrow opening. When he figured she'd had long enough to study it, he pulled it back and handed one of his smudged business cards through the crack.

The door closed. He heard the chain being undone. She opened the door halfway.

Pat Howell, one step up from Jones, looked down at the

detective with an irritated expression. She wore a white silk blouse, a pleated purple skirt, black stockings, and black high-heeled shoes.

Driver's license records had her at forty-two years of age, and Jones thought she more than looked it. Lines radiated from the corners of her eyes. Two creases bracketed her crimsoned mouth. Her makeup was heavy. She had blond hair, streaked with lighter shades, worn in two curving waves reaching to her shoulders. A Virginia Slims was stuck in one corner of her mouth, its filter red with lipstick.

She appeared to be getting ready to go out. A purple jacket to match her skirt was draped over the bottom of the banister, and she tilted her head, trying to thread an earring through her pierced ear.

"You Patricia Howell?" Jones asked.

She nodded impatiently.

"If this is about the neighborhood parking permit, I'm sorry."

She spoke in a low, raspy voice. Probably the cigarettes, Jones thought. The wrinkles too were probably from smoking. He had read that somewhere.

"I know my permit has expired. I just haven't had the time to get over to the precinct for a new one. I'll have my secretary do it first thing tomorrow morning. Promise. Okay?"

"It's not about parking," A.L. advised her.

"Well, what's it about?" Her voice was breathy and exasperated, with a faint hint of Southern origins in the way she stretched out "about."

"It's about something you don't want to talk about at your front door."

Howell frowned and motioned the detective inside. He stepped in and closed the door. She stepped back a couple of feet, but did not invite him into the sitting room that opened off the hall. Real hospitable, Jones thought. He glanced around.

The floor of the hall was white marble, or something that looked like white marble, partly covered by an Oriental rug. The stairway leading up was carpeted in a similar pattern. An ornate round gold mirror hung on the wall to Jones's left. On the right, just beyond the archway into the sitting room, was a large mahogany cabinet loaded with china, crystal, and silver.

"Well?" Howell prompted irritably.

"You ever eat lunch at . . ." He hesitated a moment, not sure he could pronounce it correctly. "Sfuzzi, Sfuzzi's restaurant in Union Station?"

"What's this about?" Pat Howell's husky voice took on a defensive tone.

"Just answer my questions, Miss Howell. Do you eat lunch every Thursday at—"

"The hell I'll answer your questions!" she flared. "I don't answer questions from cops without my lawyer."

Most of the suspects Jones questioned didn't have lawyers. At least until the judge appointed a public defender for them. Normally, the detective read them their rights, they shrugged, and he interrogated them.

"I just have a few questions. You won't need a lawyer."

"I said no lawyer, no questions."

Jones accepted the fact that he wasn't going to be able to push her or cajole her into answering.

"Who's your lawyer?"

"Solomon Greybach of Greybach, Porter, and Rothman. Eighteenth and K. Call him. He'll make an appointment."

"When?"

"I don't know!" she flared again. "Call Sol. He'll set it up."

"It's got to be tomorrow," A.L. insisted. "What time can you make it?"

"I don't know! I haven't got my calendar!" she retorted. "I've got a busy day tomorrow. I'm on the Hill all day, seeing senators and congressmen."

He guessed that was supposed to impress him.

"Got to be tomorrow."

"All right! In the afternoon. Call Sol. He'll give you a time."

She reached around him and opened the door.

"Pat?" It was a man's voice from upstairs. "Who is it? Everything all right?"

"It's all right, Kurt," Howell called. "I'll tell you later."

She closed the door hard behind Jones.

The detective walked down the metal steps of Pat Howell's house and headed back toward his car.

The door two houses away opened and a man tugging a leash attached to a ridiculously trimmed white dog started out. When he spotted Jones's black face, he retreated into the house, dragging the dog behind him. A.L. heard the deadbolt slam home and the chain rattle into its slot.

Did the whole neighborhood have an attitude? Probably.

CHAPTER TWENTY-SEVEN

GREYBACH, PORTER, AND Rothman occupied the top two floors of an office building at the corner of Eighteenth and K streets in the heart of downtown Washington. The intersection was to Washington's law, lobbying, and public relations powers what the corner of Wall Street and Broad was to the investment world.

All the office buildings along K Street were uniformly one hundred thirty feet high, limited by a local law prohibiting any structure from towering over the Washington Monument. Back in his younger days, when A.L. still hoped to become an architect, he had dreamed of designing apartment towers that would soar into the sky. He had been disappointed to learn that a squat twelve stories was all he would be allowed.

Jones arrived promptly at four P.M., the time at which a saccharine-voiced secretary had instructed him over the phone to appear for his meeting with Mr. Greybach and Ms. Howell.

The receptionist's station on the twelfth floor was a massive wood-and-brass battlement. The receptionist, a fifty-ish woman with pounds of silver jewelry, a British accent, and a smile that never faded, advised A.L. that Mr. Greybach would be with him shortly. Would he please take a seat in the waiting area. Did he wish coffee? He did. It was delivered in a delicate china cup by an elderly black woman in a traditional gray and white maid's uniform.

The detective drank the coffee and studied the notes he'd made on Patricia Howell's background. He'd spent a couple of hours the night before hunched over the computer keyboard and on the phone.

It had been easy to find out that she ran a public relations agency. No surprise there. Fit with the Georgetown lifestyle.

Her arrest record, however, did surprise Jones. Soliciting for prostitution, 1975, not prosecuted. Possession of a half gram of cocaine, 1987, not prosecuted. DWI, 1991, reduced to reckless driving.

When A.L. noticed that her birthplace was Greensboro, North Carolina, he decided to call his cousin Russell, who happened to be on the police force in Greensboro.

Cousin Russell had looked up Patricia Howell's record and reported that she had been arrested for shoplifting in her hometown in 1966 and released to her parents. Arrested for marijuana possession in 1970 and given a suspended sentence. Arrested for disorderly conduct—working as a topless dancer in a go-go joint—in 1972 and given a suspended sentence. And arrested twice for drunk driving and fined.

The detective's coffee was gone, he'd memorized his

notes, twenty minutes had passed, and still no meeting with Howell and Greybach. A.L. was getting pissed.

Keeping him waiting like this was a tactic to intimidate him, the detective decided. They thought their time was more valuable than his. And, of course, he knew it was. These big-time Washington lawyers charged $300 an hour, he'd heard. A.L. got $20.76 an hour. Plus overtime.

He was sorry now he'd worn a newly laundered white shirt and his most recently pressed suit, a conservative gray pin-striped number from Woodies. Made him feel like a Tom, trying to fit in with whitey. Should have worn an ill-fitting and mismatched coat and slacks with a wrinkled shirt and his tie pulled down. And his gun showing. Live down to their stereotypes.

Maybe if he'd shown up like that, the receptionist with the fixed smile would have whisked him right into the meeting. Get him out of the lobby before any clients could see him.

He'd give them five more minutes. Then he'd flash his badge at the receptionist and demand to see Greybach and Howell *right now*.

Just then the door to the waiting area opened and a man shaped like a bowling ball entered with his hand extended.

"Detective Jones? Sol Greybach. Sorry. Sorry. I apologize for keeping you waiting."

Solomon Greybach was overly cordial. He was in his shirtsleeves. Jones noticed how the creamy shirt draped the lawyer's girth smoothly. No pulls anywhere. Probably handmade. Couple of hundred bucks. The cufflinks were disks emblazoned with the presidential seal. Jones remembered somebody named Greybach had been something in the government of some President.

Greybach waddled ahead, leading the way. His black

trousers were held up—not that they needed holding up—by maroon and orange suspenders patterned with footballs, goalposts, and helmets. Redskins braces.

Greybach, Porter, and Rothman would have its own box at RFK Stadium, the detective guessed. For clients and politicians and journalists the firm needed to impress.

"Here we are." The lawyer waved Jones into a conference room.

Pat Howell was already there, sitting, smoking, at an oval mahogany table that filled the center of the room. A young man, also in shirtsleeves and braces, sat at the table, making notes on a yellow pad.

They'd kept him waiting because they were meeting to discuss their strategy, to get their stories straight, Jones guessed.

Around the table were a dozen high-backed armchairs, imposing as a judge's chair, upholstered in a subdued pattern of blue and gray. Along one wall stood a credenza, also mahogany, on which sat a silver coffee set, china cups and saucers, a silver ice bucket, heavy glasses, and, incongruously, a dozen cans of Coke and Diet Coke.

One wall was a window overlooking the traffic on K Street. On the other walls hung a set of related black-and-white abstract line drawings.

Jones slid into one of the high-backed chairs directly across from Pat Howell, the position he was accustomed to for an interrogation.

"Coffee? Soda?" Greybach offered.

The detective shook his head.

"So." Greybach took a seat next to his client. "Miss Howell tells me you went to her home last evening and attempted to ask her questions about her personal activities. She was, understandably, upset by your unannounced visit.

I'm sorry you didn't contact me first, Detective Jones. I've represented Miss Howell and her company for a good many years. I'd have been happy to facilitate a successful resolution to your inquiries."

"Yeah, well."

Solomon Greybach slid an engraved business card across the table to Jones.

The detective dug out his wallet. He had only one card left, and he'd scrawled a phone number on the back of it. He shrugged and stuffed the wallet back in his pocket. He pulled out his bent notebook.

Pat Howell lit another Virginia Slims with an impatient motion. She hadn't looked at Jones once since he'd come in.

"Detective Jones, will you tell me the nature of your interest in my client?" Greybach asked. "I phoned my friend Chief Jefferson this morning, and he tells me you're attached to the Homicide Squad."

That's the way with these fancy lawyers, A.L. thought. Drop a name. Try to intimidate him. Jones wondered whether Greybach had ever met a homicide detective before. Or represented a client involved in a murder investigation. What A.L. heard was that these downtown lawyers didn't practice much law. Introduced people to each other, fixed things, and gave advice, for big bucks.

A.L. didn't show the slightest reaction to Greybach's friendship with the police chief.

"Surely Miss Howell is not involved in any way in a murder investigation," the lawyer said.

"Maybe."

"Oh, for Christ's sake!" Pat Howell angrily snuffed out her cigarette.

"I need to ask her some questions."

"You may ask your questions, Detective. But I will

counsel my client as to whether
not."

"You can counsel he.
had run out of patience wit.
tion her here or downtown."

"Sol, really! This is an outr
The lawyer put a restraining .
The other lawyer was scribblin,
low pad.

"Proceed, Detective Jones," Greybac
"Miss Howell, you eat regularly at a
Sfuzzi, Sfuzzi's, in Union Station?"

She looked at Greybach. He nodded.

"I've eaten there. It's a popular place on the
"Regularly?"

"What do you mean by 'regularly'?" the lawye.
vened.

"Regularly. Like often. Like once a week."

"I don't recall how often I've eaten there," Howe,
responded through tight lips. "Not once a week, probably. I
don't recall."

The lawyer's favorite evasion. No one could prove
whether or not she could recall.

"How often?" Jones persisted. "Once every two
weeks?"

"She said she's eaten there, Detective Jones," Greybach
interjected. "I'll stipulate that she's eaten there often. Okay?"

"You eat lunch there every Thursday?" the detective
pressed.

"I don't have my calendar with me," Howell responded,
lighting another cigarette.

"You need your calendar to remind you if you eat at the
same place every Thursday?"

nk we've gone about as far as we need to go on this
tective Jones," Greybach declared.

t me ask my questions, man."

sk all you want. I'm instructing the witness . . . er,
ent not to answer any more questions about the fre-
y of her meals at Sfuzzi. She says she dines there often.
's it."

The detective let it pass.

"Where were you early on the morning of April twen-
-ninth? Around two A.M.?"

"Home in bed, I assume. But I'd have to look at my calendar to be sure. I may have been out of town."

"It was the night Curtis Davenport was murdered, if
that jogs your memory any."

"Is that what this is all about?" Solomon Greybach
jumped in. "You suspect Pat of being involved in Davenport's death? That is preposterous, Detective Jones!"

"Maybe so. But 'preposterous' ain't no answer. I'd like
to hear Miss Howell answer my question."

"I will not let—"

"I was home in bed that night," Pat Howell responded
before Greybach could stop her.

"Anybody there with you can vouch for that?"

"Yes," she replied.

The answer took Jones by surprise. He thought he saw
a smug smile twitching at the corners of her mouth.

"Who?"

"My boyfriend. Kurt Voss. K-U-R-T V-O-S-S. Check it
out."

The detective wrote the name in his notebook. He was
sure she was needling him.

"You know a man named Frog?" A.L. changed direction.

"Frog?" Pat Howell exhaled a cloud of blue smoke. "Is that his first name or his last name?"

"That's his whole name, his street name."

"I know no one named Frog."

"You sure?"

"You're badgering her." Greybach jumped in again. "She says she doesn't know anyone named Frog. Move on, please. I assume it will become obvious very soon the purpose of these questions?"

The fat fart was getting on Jones's nerves.

"Yeah, it's going to be real obvious. You know anything about selling cocaine, Miss Howell?"

"All right, Detective." Greybach hauled himself out of his deep armchair. "I think you've gone far enough."

"Want me to call for backup to take her downtown?" Jones stared down the lawyer.

Greybach dropped back into his seat. This was definitely not the type of legal work he was normally involved in.

"I will instruct my client not to answer questions I consider improper."

The detective ignored him.

"Know anything about selling cocaine?" Jones repeated his question to Howell.

"I don't use it," she spat at him.

"You stopped since your arrest?" A.L. couldn't resist needling her. "Glad to hear it."

The detective thought he saw the lawyer stiffen.

"You don't use it. But do you sell it?"

"Detective . . ." The lawyer tried to intervene. Jones pressed on.

"You ever sell it? Or get somebody else to sell it for you? Or maybe you give it away, make friends with them folks up on the Hill? Frog leave a package of powder in your car every Thursday while you're eating at Sfuzzi's?"

"No! No! No!" the woman shouted.

"I think we're done here." Greybach heaved out of his chair and lumbered toward the door. "You'll need a piece of paper with a whole lot of official writing on it before I'll let you question my client any further, Detective Jones."

Jones knew he'd blown it.

His temper got the best of him sometimes. But, hell, he was never going to get straight answers out of her anyhow. And Greybach was definitely getting under his skin. At least he'd vented his frustrations. Better than holding them in. He had read that somewhere.

The detective didn't wait to be shown out. In the waiting area, the British-accented receptionist flashed him another empty smile.

It was going-home time for workers in the building. The elevator was crowded with chattering men and women toting briefcases and canvas gym bags. Some of the women had changed their high heels for white cotton socks and jogging shoes for the walk home. They looked ridiculous, Jones thought.

He bought a can of root beer from a street vendor on K Street and leaned against the building, reviewing the frustrating session.

Patricia Howell was lying about the coke, of course. She acted guilty as hell. And if she didn't have anything to hide, why the big deal with the lawyer protecting her?

But how was he supposed to squeeze her? White bitch, connected, obviously. Dropping that she was tight with senators and congressmen. Heavy-duty white lawyer dropping the chief's name.

Jones knew he didn't have enough to haul her downtown for a real interrogation. He was sure the captain would never authorize him to bring Howell in for questioning on the say-so of Frog.

As it was, the lawyer was probably going to complain to the chief and the chief was going to complain to the captain and the captain was going to chew his ass for hassling her.

So where was he on finding out if Howell did Davenport, or had him done, to protect her Capitol Hill coke business?

No fucking where.

The detective looked at his watch. Six o'clock. Maybe he'd spend a couple of hours cruising Columbia Heights. See if he could spot a drug boy he wanted to talk to about a drive-by.

CHAPTER TWENTY-EIGHT

JANE WAS COMBING through electronic clipping files on her computer in the *Post* newsroom, reading old stories about the drug trade on Capitol Hill, searching for something, anything, that might provide a lead on Curtis's murder.

She'd been at it a couple of hours. Her eyes burned and her shoulders ached. She stood up to stretch when the phone on her desk bleated.

"Hello?"

"Hi."

The voice sounded familiar.

"It's Jerry Knight," the caller prompted. "You still mad at me from the memorial service?"

"No, Mr. Knight. I'm still mad that they give you five hours of airtime every night to inflict your views on the American people."

"Does that mean you've been listening?"

"Did you call me for some reason, Mr. Knight?"

"I read your piece about Davenport and the drug ring. So you're still covering the murder investigation?"

"I am."

"I have something to tell you about Davenport. The police aren't interested. But you seem to be really immersed in this case."

Jane instantly hit a few keys on her keyboard, clearing the clipping files off the computer screen. She tapped in JERRY KNIGHT PHONE CALL, the date and time, and prepared to take notes on the conversation.

"What is it?"

"Not over the phone. I'd prefer to give it to you face-to-face. How about dinner?"

"How about face-to-face over a cup of coffee at my office?"

"Me, at the *Washington Post*? Are you kidding? What would my fans say if they ever found out I went into the *den of the enemy*? No way!"

"Why don't you call the *Washington Times*, then, Mr. Knight? They share your political views. Tell them whatever it is you know about Curtis."

Jane hit the DEL button on her computer keyboard, erasing Knight's name, the date, and the time. There would be no notes on this conversation. She prepared to retrieve the clipping files.

"Good idea," Knight said. "I'll call the *Times*."

"I'll meet you for lunch," Jane bargained, unwilling to lose a potential story.

"I don't do lunch," Jerry replied. "I sleep all day. It's got to be dinner."

"I don't do dinner," Jane retorted. "I work for a morning paper. I'm writing at dinnertime."

"How about breakfast?" Jerry suggested. "I'll be off the

air, getting ready to go to bed. You'll be waking up, getting ready to go to work. It's the only time we're both awake and available."

"Are you kidding?" Jane shot back. "I can't stomach you when I'm fully awake. First thing in the morning? Forget it."

"Okay, listen. Here's an idea," Jerry offered. "Tomorrow night I'm scheduled to do a bit at Pat Howell's Celebrity Stand-up Comic Competition. It's that annual charity fundraiser. Cancer or blindness or something like that. Meet me there and we'll go out for a drink afterward. I'll tell you something interesting about Davenport."

"All right," she agreed grudgingly.

"Great. Madison Hotel. Come at eight o'clock. I'll see if I can make you laugh."

"Doubtful," Jane said and hung up.

CHAPTER TWENTY-NINE

THE MADISON HOTEL was a favorite stopping place for visiting dignitaries from foreign countries, especially from the Middle East. When Jerry arrived, he noticed two gray limos double-parked at the entrance. Unfamiliar flags hung from staffs on the front fenders. A State Department "war wagon," a black Chevy Suburban full of security guards and guns, was parked behind the limos. And in the small lobby, a platoon of muscular and menacing men scrutinized Jerry and everyone else who came in.

Jerry headed for the spiral staircase near the entrance to the Montpelier Room restaurant at the rear of the lobby. He climbed to the ballroom on the second floor. Pat Howell greeted him at the door.

"Sweetie! Thanks so much for agreeing to do this," she purred in her husky voice, puckering her lips in the general direction of Jerry's left cheek. Jerry inhaled her pungent perfume. She was wearing a filmy tiger-print blouse and baggy black silk trousers. "Go have a drink. I'll find you when we're ready to start."

Pat gently but firmly steered him into the room, at the same time turning away to greet the next arrival, a classic Washington maneuver.

The Madison was located across Fifteenth Street from the *Washington Post,* so Jane Day didn't have far to come. Jerry scanned the crowd but didn't see her. Her loss if she didn't show, Jerry thought.

The ballroom was set up like a cabaret, with tables and chairs arranged in front of a small stage. Above the stage hung a banner reading, TENTH ANNUAL CELEBRITY STAND-UP COMIC COMPETITION. BENEFIT D.C. DRUG REHABILITATION CENTER. In the back of the room were two bars and two tables of hors d'oeuvres.

Jerry pushed his way to one of the bars and ordered a gin martini, very dry, straight up, with a tiny onion. He prided himself on not succumbing to the white-wine-and-nonalcoholic-beer yuppie affectation. He took a deep and satisfying swallow, smacked his lips in pleasure, and looked around the room.

The comedy competition was not an A List event, like the Kennedy Center Honors or the White House Correspondents Association banquet. So the A List of Washington VIP's didn't bother to turn out. Jerry saw a couple of second-tier senators, a dozen House members, and a lot of congressional staff happy for the free food and free booze. There was just one cabinet member who was too new to Washington to know that this event was below his status.

The other two hundred or so attendees were lobbyists, lawyers, and PR types. Pat Howell had promised them face time with powerful Washington policymakers for the price of $150 a ticket.

Ten years ago, a just-divorced Howell had staged the

first Celebrity Stand-Up Comic Competition to gain visibility for her new PR firm. The event had been based on two simple premises: most of Washington's movers and shakers are hams who believe they can tell a joke as well as Jay Leno or Mark Russell, and a lot of people will pay good money to see VIPs make fools of themselves. The event had become an annual Washington ritual.

Howell caught Jerry's eye and motioned him to join the other contestants next to the little stage. This year's show was about to begin. He picked up a refill on his martini and squeezed through the tables to face the competition: a Washington Redskins lineman who doubled as a disk jockey on a local rock station, a fiftyish woman White House correspondent, an avowedly gay congressman, and a local TV anchorman who wore the most fake-looking toupee Jerry had ever seen.

Jerry figured he'd win easy, if the judging was fair. Ah, but there was the rub. This was his third year in the contest and he'd not won yet. He was sure it was because the judges were all a bunch of liberals unwilling to reward his politically incorrect humor.

He checked out the judges' table. There in the middle, glaring at Jerry, sat a humorless woman senator who had once demanded that the FCC investigate him for a remark he'd made on air about welfare mothers. Jerry knew for sure he was cooked when he noticed the senator was wearing this season's most politically correct feminist symbol, a lapel pin made from shards of broken glass. A symbol of women crashing through the glass ceiling.

The senator would never allow Jerry to win the contest. What the hell. It was for a good cause, curing drug addicts. Get 'em off the street before they could mug him. Or kill him, like Davenport.

Jerry scanned the room again. Jane Day still had not showed.

The football player went first. He was funny, Jerry had to admit, in a sophomoric way. A little dirty, which the crowd loved. He got a good round of applause.

The White House correspondent was next. She was very nervous as she related an interminable anecdote about covering President Bush's trip to Tokyo, during which he threw up on the Japanese prime minister. The place was stone silent.

Jerry followed her. Not a tough act to follow. He began with some radio show patter.

"Hello, hello, hello, you lucky people! Most of the world has to wait until midnight to hear the wit and wisdom of the greatest talk show host of them all. But you get to hear me at eight P.M.! I'm here tonight as part of an affirmative-action program, the token white, middle-aged conservative male."

This was greeted with good-natured booing and hissing.

Jerry swung into his routine, glancing down at notes he'd made on a three-by-five file card cupped in his hand.

"Tonight, I'm going to give you my list of the ten things I hate most about Washington."

Light hissing.

"Number ten: environmental kooks. Now they want to outlaw backyard barbecue grills. Next thing you know, the clean-air police will be pounding on your door. 'Okay, throw out those briquettes and come out with your hands up!' "

There was some laughter. Jerry glanced at the senator-judge. She was not amused.

"Number nine: the news reporters on NPR, who over-enunciate their words because they think the listeners are too damn dumb to understand what they're talking about."

Less laughter on that one. Better try something a little racier.

"Number eight: indecipherable sexual orientations in *Washingtonian* magazine personal ads. What the hell is a BIMFW in search of a BISME? Whatever happened to a good, old-fashioned HWM . . . horny white male?"

A lot of laughter.

Jerry spotted Jane Day standing in the back. The spotlights were in his eyes, but he could see she was not laughing. Good thing she wasn't a judge.

"Number seven: people who insist on finding a 'root cause' for every social problem. To them, the root cause is usually that I don't pay enough income taxes. To me, the root cause when some punk mugs me in the street is that he's got a gun in my ribs and wants my wallet."

Jerry didn't bother to look at the woman senator. He knew he was not going to win.

"Number six: premenstrual syndrome."

Loud boos.

"PMS. My ex-wife has had premenstrual syndrome for eight years. Nonstop. What we ought to do is get a bunch of women soldiers whose periods all come at the same time, and about three days before they're supposed to start, parachute them into Iraq. Saddam Hussein wouldn't stand a chance."

Loud sustained boos.

Jerry looked for Jane Day. Still there, and still not laughing. He continued down his list, wearying of the contest. He wondered why he subjected himself to this every year. He preferred radio, where he couldn't see the audience.

"Number two: people who lobby for Japan."

The room got quiet. A lot of people there lobbied for Japan.

"How can you like a country that steals our national sport, won't buy our products, and is destroying the brains of our children with Nintendo? I'm protesting. I'm boycotting sushi, I have a bumper sticker that says REMEMBER PEARL HARBOR, and I'm spreading the word that driving a Honda causes cancer."

Not much reaction.

"And the number one thing I hate about Washington . . . Well, I wanted to close with a really big political joke, so, number one: Congress!"

Jerry finished to mixed applause and booing. He yelled "Liberal scum," bowed extravagantly, and stepped down from the stage. He wanted to seek out Jane Day. But he was required to remain at the table until the last two contestants had completed their routines.

Finally, the winners were announced. The football player won. The anchorman was second. The gay Congressman was third.

He found Jane Day waiting at the back of the ballroom.

"How'd you like it?" he greeted her.

"Don't give up your night job."

"I'm going to put you down as 'undecided,'" Jerry joked. He thought he caught a very tiny smile.

"You said you know something about the Davenport case," Jane said. "Let's hear it."

"You get right to the point, don't you? Let's talk about it over a drink."

"It's too late for a drink."

"Too late? It's barely nine o'clock."

"Don't you have to be on the air?"

"Not until midnight."

"All right," she agreed. "One drink."

"You are truly generous," Jerry replied.

They were at the door. Pat Howell was bidding her guests good night.

"Sweetie, you were so funny," she told Jerry. "I don't know why you didn't win. Next year for sure."

Howell was staring at Jane.

Jerry introduced them. "This is Jane Day of the *Post*. Pat Howell.

Howell's penciled eyebrows arched upward.

"I've read you but I've never met you."

The two women shook hands.

"I hope you'll write something good about our fund-raiser."

"I'm not covering," Jane replied. "I came to meet Mr. Knight."

"Still at it, huh, Jerry?" Howell laughed suggestively. "Maybe the fourth time'll be the charm." She blew a kiss in his direction and turned to another departing guest.

"What did she mean, 'Maybe the fourth time'll be the charm'?" Jane asked when they were in the hotel corridor.

"I've been married three times."

"Of course. I could have guessed. Are you married now?"

"No. Why? Are you interested?"

She pantomimed gagging on a finger down her throat.

Jerry spotted a familiar figure loitering near the top of the stairs.

"Detective Jones. What are you doing here?"

"I'm working," the detective replied. "Checking some things out."

"On the Davenport case?" Jane asked.

"Can't say, Miss Day."

"You two know each other?" Jerry asked.

"We've talked," Jane replied.

The three of them stood awkwardly for a moment.

"Yeah, well. Y'all have a nice night." The detective headed toward the ballroom.

"What do you think he's really doing here?" Jerry asked as they descended the spiral staircase to the lobby.

"He suspects I've got information that I'm not sharing," Jane said. "He's snooping around to see if I'll lead him to someone."

"You think Jones is interested in that drug angle you wrote about?"

"Probably."

He started toward the dark Madison bar in a corner of the lobby.

"No way." She pulled back. "The paper's right across the street. Somebody might see us here."

"So what?"

"Me with *you*? Be serious."

"All right, let's walk over to Sam and Harry's on Nineteenth."

"I'm allergic to cigar smoke and overweight white guys in thousand-dollar suits."

"The Palm?"

"Even more overweight white guys in fifteen-hundred-dollar suits."

"All right," he said in exasperation. "You pick a place."

"The Tabard Inn on N. It's only a couple of blocks."

"The Tabard Inn?" he protested. "That's for aging hippies left over from the 1960s."

"Perfect."

CHAPTER THIRTY

SHE ORDERED A glass of white wine. He'd anticipated she would.

He ordered a gin martini, straight up, with an onion. She'd anticipated he'd drink something macho and outdated.

The Tabard Inn and the narrow tree-lined street on which it stood looked more like London than Washington. In the Victorian era, the row of four-story redbrick and white stone buildings had been the mansions of Washington's rich and famous. Now they were mostly law offices and think tanks.

The Tabard had been converted from town houses to an inn during World War I and claimed to be Washington's oldest continuously operating hostelry.

The lounge was just behind the dowdy reception area. It was a small, dark room with beamed ceiling and shoulder-high wood paneling. It was lit only by dim frosted wall sconces.

There was one round table in front of a narrow bookcase that appeared to hold a 1923 edition of *The World Book Encyclopedia*. The rest of the room was jammed with heavy Victorian sofas and overstuffed armchairs in a variety of worn upholstery.

Jane and Jerry sat side by side on a red plush sofa. Above their heads hung an engraving, PARADE OF THE GRAND ARMY OF THE REPUBLIC, SEPTEMBER 20, 1892.

They could hear the noise of the restaurant and small bar at the rear of the inn. But there were only two other people in the lounge, a young woman in T-shirt and jeans reading a paperback book and an older woman, who looked like she might be a schoolteacher on holiday, sipping sherry.

"Yeah, this is really my kind of place," Jerry said sarcastically. "You know what the original Tabard Inn was?"

"Sure," Jane replied. "It's where the pilgrims stopped in *Canterbury Tales.*"

"I like an educated woman."

"I doubt it," she replied. "Okay, now that we've got our drinks, why don't you tell me this big secret about Curtis."

Jerry took a big swallow of his martini.

"Davenport got a phone call at the studio just before he went on the air with me. It must have been important, because he asked to use a private office to return the call."

"Yeah?" Jane dug a reporter's notebook out of her oversized tapestry shoulder bag and began making notes.

"The next day, after Davenport was killed, my producer remembered the call. She thought it might have had something to do with his murder. So she dug the phone number out of the trash can."

"Who was it from?" Jane asked. She kept her eyes on Jerry, jotting down notes without looking at the pad.

"I called the number and it was the office of Jack VanDyke."

"Jacobsen's chief of staff?"

"Right."

"Hmmm," Jane murmured. "Go on."

"I told Detective Jones, but he wasn't interested, so I decided to do a little detective work on my own. I tracked down VanDyke and asked if he'd called Davenport that night."

"And?"

"He said he hadn't."

"Hmmm," Jane murmured again, studying her notes. Unconsciously she twisted a reddish-orange curl around her finger. "Keep going."

"There's not much else. As I was leaving the reception where I talked to VanDyke, I ran into a guy named Kurt Voss. Know who he is?"

"Sure. He's a lobbyist. One of his clients is Z-Chem Plastics, the outfit that bribed Jacobsen."

"Bribed? The *Post* was forced to retract your hatchet job on Jacobsen. Or is my memory faulty on that?"

"Jacobsen did take a bribe and eventually I'm going to prove it. So cut the sarcasm and tell me what Voss said to you."

"He was drunk. Big-time drunk. I don't remember his exact words but it was something like 'I'm glad Davenport was killed, he deserved to die, and I'm sorry I didn't kill him myself.' "

Jane scribbled frantically in her pad.

"And?"

"That's all. Voss staggered away and I left."

The reporter sat back in her corner of the well-worn

sofa and studied her notes, flipping back and forth through the pages in the dim light. She absently took a swallow of wine. Jerry signaled the waitress for another.

Jane seemed more relaxed now, Jerry thought. Maybe it was the wine, or her gratitude for the information he'd given her.

"Why'd you decide to become a reporter?" he asked, lapsing into his interviewer mode.

Maybe it was the wine. Maybe it was the setting, more cozy parlor than bar. Maybe she just wanted to put off going back to an empty apartment. Whatever. As she worked her way through the second glass of wine, she told him her life story. Born in L.A., an only child, father a lawyer, mother a doer of good deeds who lived vicariously through her daughter's career.

Her decision to become a journalist had been born of Watergate. She was fourteen years old when Nixon resigned.

Fourteen in 1974, Jerry calculated. So she was born in 1960. Mid-thirties now. No wedding ring.

Watergate was the nightly topic of dinner-table conversation at home, Jane rambled on. Her parents thought Nixon and his gang were devils incarnate. And so did she.

"You people never give up, sticking it to him, do you?" Jerry interjected.

She went on reminiscing dreamily, ignoring him. She was inspired to become a journalist by Woodward and Bernstein, by the vision of toppling some future President, of exposing corrupt political leaders who betrayed the voters, who were bought and paid for by the fat cats, who ignored the needs of the needy.

"Who'll play your part in the movie?" Jerry asked to deflate the rhetoric. "Bernadette Peters?"

She rolled on. English degree from Brown. First real job at a community paper in San Francisco. Then Berkeley, where she'd earned her master's while free-lancing for Pacifica Radio and the *Los Angeles Times.*

"A doctorate from Harvard," Jerry interjected, "and you'd score a perfect one hundred on the liberal education scoreboard."

She ignored him and continued to summarize her life story.

Five years at the *Atlanta Constitution,* where she was assigned to the legislative beat and later to environmental issues. And three years at the *Washington Post,* recruited during one of the paper's periodic efforts to hire more women. Assigned first to the Metro desk, covering local news of Washington and its suburbs. Later promoted to backup reporter on the environmental beat. The Jacobsen story was her first big national story. And . . .

Jane's voice trailed off. She gulped the last of the wine.

"What about you?" she demanded, sitting forward suddenly on the sofa. "Is it true you are the illegitimate son of Ronald Reagan?"

Jerry laughed hard at her unexpected humor.

"My life has been one long saga of cheering for the overdog. None of that bleeding-heart sympathy for the underdog for me."

He looked at his watch.

"But my long, hard climb to the top is going to have to be for another night. I've got a radio show to do. Millions of Americans are waiting anxiously."

Jane realized that her attitude toward Jerry had softened. He was outrageously egotistical, of course. And a far-out conservative. But up close he seemed a harmless eccentric. He could be funny. And he seemed truly interested in her. Which was more than she could say for most of the men she met.

She insisted on paying for her drinks. While they waited for the waitress to return with their credit card receipts, Jane returned to business.

"Can I get a tape of your interview with Curtis?" she asked. "Maybe I'll hear something. I don't know, maybe something that will explain the phone call from VanDyke."

"Sure. We record the show every night. My loyal fans can't get enough of me so they order the tapes. The usual charge is nine ninety-five. But for you, free."

"It's my lucky night. I must have had a good horoscope."

"I'm on my way to the studio now. Walk over with me. It's only a couple of blocks. I'll give you the tape."

CHAPTER THIRTY-ONE

Leaving the Tabard, they turned right on N and left at the corner onto Eighteenth Street. At Connecticut and M, they passed a little triangular park whose shadows were inhabited at this hour by the dark shapes of homeless men wrapped in tattered blankets.

"Aren't you afraid?" Jane twitted Jerry. "I thought you conservatives were paranoid about street crime."

"I'm not afraid as long as I've got my Mace."

"You carry Mace?"

"Sure. Don't you?"

Jerry pulled open his suit jacket and showed her a cylinder twice the size of a pen clipped to his inside pocket.

"But it's against the law," Jane said.

"The next time you get mugged, I'm sure the emergency-room nurses will be very impressed that you obeyed the law. I'm fighting back. I'm not going to let myself become a victim."

"And I guess you carry a gun, too," she said.

"Right." Jerry lifted his briefcase to show her where his gun was hidden.

"I should have known you'd be a gun nut."

"Why 'gun nut'? Because I want to protect myself, because I refuse to be a victim? The nutty part is that the law-abiding citizens in this city are the prisoners in their homes while the criminals are roaming free. You wouldn't be walking on M Street right now, at eleven o'clock at night, if I weren't with you."

"If we dealt with the root causes of crime, if we provided meaningful jobs—"

"Give me a break!" Jerry cut in. "It's after hours. You don't have to sound like the *Washington Post* editorial page."

"Well, Mace and guns are not the answer," she insisted.

"Maybe not. But I like to think of them as the 'root causes' of my survival."

CHAPTER THIRTY-TWO

AFTER JANE GOT the tape, she went straight back to the *Post*.

The newsroom was mostly deserted. Russ was still at his desk. The night staff was stoking up in the coffee room.

Jane slapped the cassette into the machine on her desk. She was intrigued by Jerry's revelation of the phone call from VanDyke's office. She hoped the tape contained some clue about the murder. She needed a break to redeem her career at the *Post*.

Jane pressed the play button.

"Don't you people realize . . ."

It was Jerry's voice in her earphones, somehow less abhorrent, more entertaining now that she'd spent an evening over drinks with him.

". . . the automobile—yes, the automobile you hate so much—gives Americans the freedom to move to a better house in the suburbs, to commute to good-paying jobs, to take the family for a picnic in the country on the weekends, or a vacation at the beach. Don't you consider those worth-while social values?"

"Of course they are—"

It shocked her to hear Curtis's earnest voice again.

"—but public transportation can carry people all those places without polluting our air."

"Public transportation!" Jerry hooted. "When was the last time *you* rode a bus?"

"We recently had a fund-raiser and the guests were transported from a black-tie dinner at the Mayflower to a concert at the Kennedy Center by chartered bus," Davenport replied in a tone of triumph, not realizing the trap he'd fallen into.

"A thousand-bucks-per-person fund-raiser and the guests rode the bus!" Jerry boomed. "Just like real, common, everyday, ordinary people! We'll be back with more from this down-to-earth bus rider after these commercial messages."

Jane pressed fast forward.

The recording of the show went on and on, Jerry Knight making fun of environmental concerns and Curtis explaining in his even, reasonable manner.

Jane was losing her concentration. She started reading press releases and notes on other stories.

Suddenly her attention snapped back to the tape. She stopped it, rewound for a few seconds, then hit play. She'd heard something.

". . . let's not get too philosophical here, Curtis," Jerry said on the recording. "It's really a simple question. How far should we go in protecting planet Earth, as you like to call it?"

"What about obeying the laws already on the books?" Curtis's voice suggested. "What about insisting that

Corporate America stop buying off politicians and others who profess to believe in environmentalism so it can continue to pile up unconscionable profits from polluting our planet?"

"Ah ha! So now we see your real target," Jerry exclaimed. "It's not pollution at all. It's the free-enterprise system, isn't it?"

The host gleefully diverted his guest into an argument over statism versus individual freedom. Jane stopped the tape recorder.

She had found a clue.

He had talked about—she checked her notes—"Corporate America buying off politicians." That must have been a reference to the Jacobsen story. Jacobsen, or more likely VanDyke, must have heard Curtis, thought his remark represented a threat to expose the Z-Chem payoff, and waited in the garage to kill him to keep him from revealing it. They didn't know Curtis had already leaked the story to her and it would be in the *Post* the next morning.

Jane recalled Jennifer Hurst's words at the wake. "Your story may have gotten Curtis killed," the woman had told her. "Jacobsen has powerful friends. His henchman, VanDyke, is like a Mafia hitman."

Jane recoiled at the idea that she could have been indirectly responsible for Curtis's death. She needed a reality check. A reality check with someone older, wiser, and less involved. She asked Russ to come to her cubicle.

She told him about the phone call to Davenport from Jacobsen's chief of staff. And she played him the portion of the cassette where Curtis talked about buying off politicians.

"Damn it, Jane," Russ barked, "you know you're not supposed to go *near* the Jacobsen story. Didn't you bring us enough grief already? If Scoffield finds out, you're gone."

"I'm *not* going near the Jacobsen story. I'm assigned to cover Curtis's murder. I just stumbled on this Jacobsen angle."

Russ listened to the tape again.

"The timing doesn't work," he finally told her. "You called Jacobsen's office for comment just before deadline, right? Got some half-ass denial? So Jacobsen and VanDyke knew we were running the story five or six hours before Davenport went on the Jerry Knight show, let's say at least five hours before VanDyke's mysterious phone call to the studio. So Davenport's reference to 'buying off' politicians didn't come as any big revelation to them."

Jane looked deflated.

"Plus, the first edition of the paper is on sale around nine o'clock," she realized. "My phone call for comment alerted Jacobsen's office the story was coming. They must have had someone waiting to pick up an early edition the minute it came off the press. Which means they'd read my story almost three hours before Davenport went on the air. So his reference to paying off politicians was old news to them by then."

Jane felt stupid. Russ turned away and started back toward his editor's desk.

"Wait. Listen, Russ." She had another idea. "Obviously Jacobsen's office did know about the story hours before Curtis went on the air. But they didn't know he was the source. Jacobsen or VanDyke hear him on Jerry Knight's show, they hear him talking about buying off politicians, they put two and two together, they realize he's the source of my story, and they kill him in retaliation."

First Fuss looked stunned. Then he looked angry.

"Jane! Give it up! You blew the Jacobsen story. Accept

it. You can't redeem yourself by pursuing this outlandish crusade to link Jacobsen to Davenport's murder."

She had no response.

"You going to be around a while?" he asked.

"I don't know. Maybe."

"Buy you a drink?"

Drinks with Jerry Knight and Russ Williamson both in one night?

"Sorry, Russ. I've got to relieve the cat sitter."

CHAPTER THIRTY-THREE

A. L. JONES RETURNED to Homicide at midnight.

He'd spent the evening in the Petworth section, off Georgia Avenue, trying to find the robber who'd pumped three bullets into a seventy-two-year-old Korean grandmother. She'd been minding her son's convenience store so the son and daughter-in-law could attend their children's school play.

Back in the office, A.L. found a yellow note stuck to his computer screen.

DAVENPORT?

It was signed by Captain Wheeler.

A.L. needed coffee.

They usually left him alone, without a partner, working his own hours. Partly because he preferred it that way, partly because the work load was too heavy to assign two guys to the same case.

The coffee was awful. He drank it anyhow.

"Davenport?" the captain's reminder prodded.

A.L.'s trip to Bull Feathers had produced nothing useful. And he wasn't going to get any more out of Patricia Howell. Or out of Frog, either. He needed to talk to Davenport's girlfriend.

He needed more puzzle pieces.

The body. Maybe the body would tell him something.

The detective reached for his phone and called William Wu at the D.C. Medical Examiner's Office.

"Hey, Willie. You still working?."

"Sure I'm working. Working the graveyard shift."

There was a high-pitched laugh at the other end of the phone line.

"Wanna come over and talk to you about a case," the detective informed him when the laugh faded.

"Yeah? What case?"

"Davenport."

"Davenport? We got a lot of cases, A.L. I don't—"

"White guy. Head beaten in on M Street, in a parking garage, about ten days ago."

"Okay. I remember now. I looked at that one myself."

"You going to be there a while?"

"I ain't going nowhere. And neither are my patients."

Another high-pitched laugh.

"See you in a little while."

It was a long drive along Massachusetts Avenue from the Municipal Center to the morgue. And it wasn't along the "good" half of Massachusetts Avenue.

A.L.'s ride was southeast along the bad half of Massachusetts Avenue, through increasingly more rundown and dangerous neighborhoods, dead-ending at Nineteenth

Street Southeast. A complex of redbrick buildings included the D.C. General Hospital for the city's sick poor, the D.C. Jail for the incarcerated poor, and the D.C. Medical Examiner's Office for the dead poor.

A.L. parked his car and entered the reception area of the Medical Examiner's Office. Two black women, one old, one young, sat on a sofa hugging each other and sobbing. Just identified the body of a relative, the detective assumed.

He peered through the small glass window in the door separating the reception area from the work area. He spotted Willie Wu bent over a metal table examining a corpse. Willie was wearing baggy blue hospital pants and a T-shirt with the letters OCME stenciled across the back: Office of the Chief Medical Examiner.

A.L. poked his head in.

"Hey, Willie. I'll wait for you out here."

The detective just didn't feel like looking at dead bodies tonight. He idly leafed through a three-month-old *Time* magazine.

The grieving women departed and eventually Willie emerged from the work area. He'd removed his latex gloves and his mask. He carried a folder of papers.

"Busy?" A.L. asked.

"Very busy," the Chinese autopsy technician replied. "People dying to get in here."

Again the laugh.

"We got fifty-five shelves in the cooler," Wu explained, sobered now. "They're all full tonight. We got to put bodies on the floor."

A.L. shook his head.

"So, you examined Davenport."

"Yeah, I did that one myself."

"And?"

"Died from multiple blows to the head." Wu consulted his folder. "You want to know exactly which parts of the brain were affected?"

"No."

"No other injuries. No murder weapon found."

"Drugs?"

"No sign."

"Alcohol?"

"A little." The technician looked in his file again. "He was killed, what, two A.M.? Three A.M.? Probably a beer for dinner. Something like that."

"That's it? That's all you got, Willie? I need something else. I need *something* on this one."

"I found some paint," Wu offered. "Maybe that'll help."

"Paint?"

"Found a couple of specks of paint imbedded in his forehead. Could of picked them up from the garage floor. But they were pretty deep. I think they came off the murder weapon."

"What color paint?"

"They're just small specks. But I checked them under a magnifier. They're green."

"What kind of paint?" A.L. pressed.

"I ran a quick test. It's just ordinary paint, as far as I can tell. Something you'd buy at Hechinger's, or any drugstore."

"And the weapon?"

"No idea." Wu leafed through his notes again. "Some kind of club or stick, I'd guess. From the look of the contusions on his skin, I'd say more likely wood than metal. That's all I know. I didn't have a lot of time to spend on it. There's so many—"

"I know. I know."

A.L. got up to leave.

"Come back again soon, A.L.," Wu said. "We got a real cool bunch down here."

The detective closed the door on the technician's unnerving cackle.

CHAPTER THIRTY-FOUR

SIX O'CLOCK IN the morning.

Jerry Knight was in his Rosslyn apartment, padding around in worn leather slippers, wearing only a maroon Redskins jersey and jockey shorts, going through his daily post-show routine.

At the end of his walk home from the studio, he'd stopped at the front desk to pick up the *Post* and the *Washington Times,* the capital's mostly ignored other paper whose conservative slant appealed to Jerry.

Now, he fetched his two morning beers, dropped onto the dark blue sofa facing the glass wall with its dramatic vista of Washington, put his feet up on the coffee table, and started through the papers.

Nothing from Jane Day about Davenport's murder.

We've lost our capacity for outrage, Jerry raged to himself. A nationally known figure is beaten to death on a downtown street in the nation's capital, and in a week his murder has disappeared from our consciousness.

Replaced by the newest atrocity. A man high on PCP had taken his ex-girlfriend and her infant daughter hostage in an apartment near Malcolm X Park, put the barrel of his .357 magnum in the baby's mouth and blown her head apart. Then he'd done the same to himself. The *Post* buried the story in the Metro section, Jerry noted.

He flung the newspaper aside in disgust. He drained the last of the beer, drew the heavy blackout curtains in the bedroom, and climbed into bed.

The phone rang, breaking his routine.

"Are you in bed with one of your bimbos?" the caller screeched without greeting. It was The Bitch, his ex-wife.

"Lila, how delightful to hear from you."

"Cut the bullshit, you son of a bitch!" Her decibel level was rising. Jerry edged the phone away from his ear. "I can hear her giggling in the background!"

"Lila, there is no one else here. I'm trying to get some sleep. What do you want? Is it Marty?"

"No! Your precious son is staying out of trouble. For a change. No thanks to you. You've fucked that kid's head up so bad!"

Jerry held the phone farther from his ear.

"If it's not Marty, then it must be money. How much do you want this time?"

"I don't need your goddamn money!" she shouted, the volume going up. "I'm making plenty of money from my decorating business!"

"Decorating? I thought you were in the antiques business? And before that, weren't you selling health foods?"

"Well, now I'm in the decorating business! And my customers like my taste! Which you never did!"

"No accounting for taste."

"What!"

"Lila, I'm trying to sleep. What do—"

"I need your car!"

"My car?"

"I need to borrow your car! Mine won't start and I've got to meet a client! I'm late!"

"Ever hear of taxis?"

"The client's in Annapolis! It's a big job! You sleep all day! You don't need your car! Why can't you lend it to me! You've given it to your bimbo, haven't you! You bastard!"

She was in full shriek now.

"Lila, I'm hanging up now. Have a nice day."

"You bastard!" She started sobbing. "You are . . . so cold. Mr. Big-time . . . radio star. You've got . . . everything and I've got nothing . . . son . . . together . . . life . . . nothing . . . trying so hard . . . you . . . ."

She was wailing incoherently.

Jerry had learned to handle her screaming. But her crying turned him sympathetic every time. And she knew it.

"Okay, Lila. Listen. Stop crying. Come on now. Stop crying. Listen to me, Lila. I'll lend you my car. Stop crying now. You know where my space is. I'll leave the keys at the front desk. Just have it back by six o'clock."

"I'll come up to your apartment and get the keys," she said, instantly recovering her composure.

"No you won't," Jerry said firmly.

He was disgusted at himself for letting Lila manipulate him again. But he wasn't going to let her talk her way into his apartment. She'd come over a couple of months before, on the pretext of delivering some mail. Once inside, she'd rampaged through the apartment looking for an imagined girlfriend. When she hadn't found anyone, she'd smashed dishes and glasses before storming out.

"I'll leave the keys at the front desk, Lila. Take it or leave it."

"You bastard!"

CHAPTER THIRTY-FIVE

THE EXPLOSION ROCKED the apartment building and startled Jerry awake.

Groggy, he didn't know what had happened. The room was dark and silent. He pushed back his black sleep mask and looked at the lighted digital numbers on the bedside clock.

Eight-fifteen.

He lay there, trying to figure out what had awakened him. A loud noise. An ominous swaying. Maybe it was a plane crash. The apartment was under the landing path for National Airport. Maybe the apartment's boiler had blown up. Maybe it was just a workman doing something.

He heard a siren far away.

Jerry got out of bed and pulled aside the blackout curtains. His eyes shut against the unaccustomed daylight. Eventually he was able to squint into the brightness. A column of black smoke was rising about fifty feet to the left. The siren noise got closer.

Uh-oh.

Jerry grabbed a robe from behind the bathroom door. He went out on the balcony, still squinting against the light. He looked down, at the source of the column of smoke.

A car in the parking lot was on fire. It was his car.

CHAPTER THIRTY-SIX

Hey, A.L."

The detective was at his battered metal desk in the grimy Homicide offices at the Municipal Center. He was slurping cold, bitter coffee from a paper cup.

After his visit to Willie Wu at the morgue, Jones had gone home and slept for a few hours. Now, he was back in the office, working the phones, trying to find out if any of his eyes knew who fired seventeen bullets into an unidentified black man in an alley off West Virginia Avenue across from Gallaudet College for the Deaf.

"Hey, A.L. I'm calling you, honey."

It was Jonetta, the dispatcher in Homicide.

"Yeah? Whadaya want?"

"Ain't you been talking to that radio dude with the mouth, Jerry Knight, about the Davenport case?"

"Yeah. What about him?"

"I'm listening to the scanner. Sounds like he just got himself blowed up."

A.L. put aside his paperwork and walked over to Jonetta's desk to listen to the scanner. An explosive device had blown up under the hood of Knight's car when the vehicle was started in the parking lot of his apartment building. There was one injured, not identified.

When he'd heard enough, the detective put on his jacket and started toward the elevator.

"That's Virginia, honey," Jonetta called after him. "That ain't our jurisdiction."

"Fuck the jurisdiction."

CHAPTER THIRTY-SEVEN

A.L. DECIDED TO try I-395 to the Fourteenth Street Bridge. He'd be going against rush hour traffic so maybe it would be fast. Cross the Potomac into Virginia, then the GW Parkway to Route 50 into Rosslyn and Jerry Knight's apartment.

While he drove, the detective tried out different scenarios for the bombing. It didn't sound like an accident from what he'd heard on the police scanner. Definite indication of explosives planted under the hood.

Maybe somebody didn't like Knight's conservative bullshit on the radio. Somebody? Hell, half the country hated his guts from what A.L. heard. But what was it Knight had said? In Washington nobody kills because of political disagreements. Character assassination maybe, but not murder.

Yeah, but hadn't some talk-show dude out west been killed by a right-wing nut case? Yeah, they made a movie out of it, A.L. recalled.

Well, if the pieces made that picture, it was an Arlington County case and the cops there were welcome to it.

The detective stomped down hard on the brake pedal to avoid hitting a car whose impatient driver swerved into his lane. Sometimes A.L. wished he was on traffic detail.

He tried the jigsaw pieces in a different order.

Big coincidence. Davenport is dropped right after he's on Knight's show, then somebody tries to drop Knight. What if the car bomb had something to do with the Davenport murder? Suppose the crackhead who busted Davenport thinks Knight knows who he is. So he goes after Knight so Knight can't ID him.

But a crackhead wouldn't use a car bomb.

Maybe it wasn't a random street thing after all. Jones turned that jigsaw piece over in his mind, and reluctantly decided it might fit.

Once he accepted that possibility, things got real complicated.

What if that girl newsie's squib in the *Post* about Davenport was true? What if some dealers on the Hill thought Davenport was going to expose them? The dealers might have shut him down before he could carry out his threat.

But did the newsie somehow tie in to Knight and his car blowing up? Jones had seen Knight and her together at that comedy thing. So there might be a connection.

He was at the Virginia end of the Fourteenth Street Bridge, making the sharp right turn down the ramp to the GW Parkway, when the thought hit him. If somebody came after Knight because he knows something about the Davenport murder, they might come after the girl newsie too for the same reason.

Jones grabbed the radio, intending to dispatch a car to protect the girl. But he couldn't remember her name. He dug his notebook out of his jacket pocket with one hand while steering with the other. He flipped through the crumpled pages.

There it was. Jane Day.

He ordered the dispatcher to find her address, send a car, and keep a watch on her until he got there.

CHAPTER THIRTY-EIGHT

THE STREET BESIDE Knight's apartment building was blocked by a jumble of fire trucks and police cars, and several TV remote trucks with their transmission masts raised high into the air.

Jones parked his car behind an Arlington County cruiser, showed his badge, and headed for the still-smoldering wreckage.

The hood, curled and blackened like a rotten banana peel, was on the roof. The windshield was gone. The fire had incinerated the rubber tires, so the wreckage hunkered on the four steel rims. It was no longer possible to tell what color the car had been. The flames had cooked off the paint, leaving a blackened hulk with the metal showing through.

The detective was surprised to see Knight standing near the demolished car, talking to a policeman, apparently unhurt. Jerry looked as though he'd dressed in a hurry. He wore a wrinkled button-down shirt, a pair of khaki slacks, and white tennis shoes with no socks.

"Hey, Detective Jones," Knight called to him. "What are you doing here?"

"Heard about it on the radio. Came to see what happened. You weren't in the car?"

"Nope. My ex-wife had borrowed my car. Reminds me of that old joke. You know, the definition of 'mixed feelings'? When you see your mother-in-law drive off a cliff in your new Mercedes."

Jones recognized the symptoms. People have a close call, they get pumped up with adrenaline, get psyched because they're still alive, start talking all kinds of inappropriate trash.

"She hurt?" the detective asked.

"A little. Not much. Only the good die young."

The Arlington policeman laughed, got Jerry to autograph his notepad, and walked away.

"You try to blow up your ex-wife?" A.L. asked Knight.

"You're kidding, right? You're joking." Jerry was incredulous. "You don't think I tried to kill Lila. Do you?"

"I never joke about killing," the detective replied in his deep rumble. "Either you tried to blow her up—sounds like you ain't real fond of her—or else somebody tried to blow you up and got her by mistake. Either way, it's attempted murder, and it ain't no joke."

"You people are unbelievable," Jerry retorted angrily. "Every teenage kid in Washington is running around the streets with an automatic weapon killing people, and you're over here in Arlington trying to nail a respectable middle-aged radio personality for attempted murder."

"Well, if you did it, you're Arlington's problem, not D.C.'s. If the bombing had anything to do with Davenport's murder, it's my problem."

"You think there's a tie-in?"

"You been sticking your nose into that case? You think the cops are too dumb to find the killer, so you're going to find him yourself, right, Mr. Night Talker?"

"I'm a radio talk-show host," Knight replied. "I'm not an amateur detective."

"Maybe whoever did Davenport found out you're snooping around," Jones speculated. "Maybe he's worried you're on to him, so he tried to take you down."

"I thought you were buying the street-violence story." Knight had quickly come down from his adrenaline high. He sounded subdued now.

"Yeah. Maybe it was, maybe it wasn't."

The two men watched firemen as they finished hosing down the remains of Jerry's car.

"Let's go for a ride," the detective suggested.

"That sounds like a line from a bad movie. You taking me in for questioning?"

"I'm taking you with me to see that girl newsie. She's been trying to tie the Davenport case to coke dealers. Not too good for her health. I saw you two together that night you made a fool of yourself at the Madison. I—"

"A fool of myself?"

"—want to find out what you two are up to."

"Come on, Detective Jones. I worked all night. I got about an hour's sleep before this happened." Jerry gestured toward the wreckage of his car. "It's way past my bedtime. I get cranky when I don't get my beauty sleep."

"I ain't got time to argue with you, Mr. Night Talker." Jones turned away. "I've got to get to that newsie's place. If somebody tried to bust you for poking into the Davenport case, they might try to bust her, too."

"Okay, I'm coming."

CHAPTER THIRTY-NINE

AT JANE DAY'S apartment in Adams-Morgan, they found a fat detective named Martinez engrossed in her *Cosmopolitan* magazines, and the reporter, still in her jogging clothes, protesting loudly that she was being held illegally without a warrant.

Jones sent Martinez away.

"What do you want?" Jane demanded of Jones. "And what's *he* doing here?"

"This conversation is off the record," the detective informed her.

"The hell it is!" Jane retorted. "You hold me prisoner in my own apartment. Your sidekick won't let me phone the lawyers at the *Post*. And you try to hide behind 'off the record'? No way! Whatever you've got to say, I'm printing every damn word in the paper."

Jane grabbed a notepad and ballpoint pen from a desk in the tiny kitchen.

"You damn reporters!" the detective growled. He glared at her for a moment. Then he spoke in a menacing tone.

"I'm trying to find out who killed your friend Curtis Davenport."

Jane stared into the detective's face, dark and grim. The corner of his left eye twitched.

"Maybe Davenport wasn't busted by a crackhead," Jones said in a voice so low it was almost drowned out by the street noises from outside. "Maybe it was something else."

"Go on," Jane said.

"Somebody put a bomb in Mr. Knight's car this morning," the detective continued. "Maybe whoever busted Davenport put the bomb in the car 'cause he thinks Mr. Knight is on his trail."

"Fortunately, only my ex-wife Lila was hurt," Jerry joked. No one laughed.

"And your stories in the newspaper might make the killer think you're on his trail, too," the detective said to Jane.

Jane withdrew a bottle of Evian water from the refrigerator and flopped down onto the floor, her back against the wall.

"So, what do you want from me?" she asked irritably.

"I think you two are doing some private investigating," the detective said. "I saw you together at the Madison. I want to know what you know about this case that I don't know."

Jane and Jerry exchanged a look. They didn't speak, but the look said: don't tell him anything.

"Damn it!" the detective cursed them. "Tell me what you're up to. Help me find out what the hell's going on."

"I'm covering the murder for the *Post*," Jane replied,

taking a swig from her water bottle. "I ask people questions. I gather information, and they print what I find out in the paper. Do I know who killed Curtis? No."

"And you?" Jones turned to Jerry Knight.

"I told you a couple of days after the murder that Davenport received a phone call just before he went on my show, but you weren't interested," Knight recalled derisively.

"So you checked it out yourself," the detective guessed.

"When you weren't interested, I checked it out myself," Jerry conceded.

"And?"

"The call was made from the office of Jack . . . James VanDyke. V-A-N-D-Y-K-E. He's chief of staff to Senator Barton Jacobsen."

Jones wrote it down in his notebook. Damn. Another white dude he'd have to question. And a redneck bigot, too. He'd seen VanDyke on TV.

"Yeah. What else have you been checking out yourself?" the detective asked.

"Nothing," Knight replied. "That's it."

"You two ain't working together?" the detective asked, looking back and forth between Jane and Jerry. "You two ain't playing detective?"

"I've said everything I have to say," Jane informed A.L., rising to her feet. "You've got any more questions, call the *Post* lawyers. I've got to get ready for work now."

"And I've got to go home and go to sleep," Jerry said.

He and Jane exchanged another look. It said: call me.

"This ain't no damn game—"

The walkie-talkie on Jones's belt squawked.

"Say again?" he spoke into the device.

More static that neither Jane nor Jerry could make out.

"I'll be right there," the detective told the caller.

Jane and Jerry looked at him expectantly.

"They just caught the guy killed Davenport," A.L. informed them.

CHAPTER FORTY

WHEN A.L. ARRIVED at Homicide, the suspect was being questioned. The presumed murderer didn't look like much.

An emaciated white guy, probably forty-five, but hard to tell. Dirty. Matted black hair. Wearing torn work pants and a gray T-shirt that had probably been white once. An old camouflage fatigue shirt.

Zonked out on booze or drugs or both. And scared witless.

"I didn't kill nobody, man. I didn't kill nobody. Man, I'm telling you, I didn't kill nobody," he jabbered incessantly.

His bloodshot eyes rolled wildly. His body trembled, from fear or addiction.

Another officer handed A.L. a report.

"The guy was spotted drunk and asleep on the sidewalk at Twenty-third and L about six A.M. by a uniformed cop on cruiser patrol. No home. No ID."

The officer pointed to a wallet on the table in front of him.

"The wallet belongs to Curtis Davenport. We found it in the pocket of this guy's pants. We've also got a parking-lot attendant at the ATN studios who remembers finding the bum asleep in the garage one morning a couple of weeks ago."

"What's your name?" A.L. asked the suspect, taking over the interrogation.

"Harry."

"Harry what?"

The suspect concentrated hard, trying to remember.

"K-K-K-Kruk. Harry Kruk."

"Crook? Harry the Crook? That's your name?"

Harry didn't get the joke.

"Where do you live, Harry?"

"Different places. I got a sister out in . . . out in . . . I forget. Sometimes I stay in the shelter. Sometimes I stay on the street. Things not too good for me right now, you know."

"Yeah, I'd say things not too good for you right now. Why'd you whack that guy in the garage, Harry?"

"I didn't whack no guy!" Harry grew more agitated, trembling violently. "I swear! I didn't whack no guy! I never killed nobody! I swear!"

"Then how come you had his wallet on you?" A.L.'s voice sounded harder.

"I found it. I found it in a trash can."

"What trash can?"

"A trash can. I don't know what trash can. I was looking for food, you know, looking in the trash cans for something to eat. The trash can was around them hotels, I think. Them hotels on M?"

"So why'd you keep it?"

"I thought somebody might give me something for it."

"What about the money in it? Whatja do with the money?"

"Wasn't no money in it. I looked."

"The credit cards?"

"I don't use credit cards."

Harry tried a smile. Jones was disgusted by the sight of his teeth.

The detective moved around behind the suspect, leaned down, and screamed into his ear.

"You are a fucking liar, Harry! You whacked that guy in the garage! You took his goddamn wallet! You spent the money on booze and dope! And you're too goddamn dumb to get rid of the evidence! Admit it, you scumbag! Stop lying, you son of a bitch!"

It was supposed to scare him into confessing.

But it didn't work.

"I didn't! I swear! I never killed nobody, man! Never! I never did! I never did it, man! I swear!

Harry was trembling uncontrollably. A dark spot spread out from the crotch of his torn trousers. He'd peed in his pants.

"Jesus!"

A.L. left the interrogation room.

This was going to go down good, Jones thought. Guy's white. Ain't got no connections. Ain't got no downtown lawyer. Ain't friends with no reporters. And he's caught with the evidence on him.

Simple.

Too simple.

In A.L.'s experience, when the puzzle pieces went together this simple, something was wrong.

"Book the fuck," Jones instructed, nevertheless.

CHAPTER FORTY-ONE

WHEN JERRY ARRIVED at the ATN studios that night for his show, he was tired and in a foul mood. More foul than usual.

The events of the morning had upset his routine. He hated to have his routine upset. He hadn't slept well. Even a third warm beer hadn't helped.

At the studio, Jerry found K. T. Zorn chuckling over something in the early edition of the next day's *Washington Post*.

"What's so funny?" Jerry asked the diminutive producer.

She held up the front page of Style, the section devoted to culture, entertainment, gossip, and self-absorbed personal journalism. The lead story was about the bombing of Jerry's car.

The headline read EVEN PARANOIDS HAVE REAL ENEMIES.

Predictably, Jerry was outraged.

"I'm outraged! Somebody tries to blow me up and they put it in Style, right above Art Buchwald. The *Post* thinks it's entertaining? And where do they get off calling me a 'paranoid'?"

"Ask them yourself," K.T. suggested. "You had a call from the *Post* about an hour ago."

The producer searched for the pink message form.

"Here it is. Jane Day. Called at nine-forty-five."

"Jane Day called me here?"

K.T. recognized the tone. She'd heard it enough times before. Jerry had another woman in his sights. She scratched her gray crew cut. He was more insufferable than usual when he was in one of these I-just-met-the-woman-of-my-dreams phases.

Jerry went into his office and closed the door. Jane answered after the first ring.

"How come you're still at the paper?" Jerry asked.

"Because I'm working on a story," she replied brusquely. "Where have you been? I've been trying to reach you for hours."

"I didn't know you cared."

"I need your comment. I've missed the early edition, but I can get it into the later editions."

"Comment on what?"

"Are you kidding? Don't you remember Jones running out of my place? They caught the guy who killed Curtis."

Jane told him what she knew about Harry Kruk and the circumstances of his capture.

"You want my response?" Jerry asked. "You want a quote? Okay, quote this: 'I'm glad our magnificent Metropolitan Police Department has managed to catch one murderer. Only about seven thousand more and it'll be safe to walk the streets again.' "

He heard her groan as she tapped his comment into her computer.

"That's what you want to say? Fine. Very classy. There's just time to get it in the home edition."

Jerry wanted to prolong the conversation.

"You think this guy really did it?" he asked before she could hang up.

"You don't?"

"It's too easy. What about Davenport's threat in the bar? What about Voss saying he was glad Davenport was dead? What about someone planting a bomb in my car? The police ignore all that. They said from the beginning it was a routine street crime, and surprise, surprise, it turns out to be a routine street crime. Sorry. It's way too simple."

"Sometimes the simple answer is the right answer. Just because you're paranoid—"

"That reminds me! I want to file a complaint about that story on the car bombing in the Style section."

"Sorry, not my department."

CHAPTER FORTY-TWO

J ERRY DEVOTED THE opening segment of the *Night Talker* show to the bombing of his car and the capture of Kruk.

"They can't silence me!" Jerry proclaimed into the microphone as soon as the red ON AIR sign lit up.

"Yes, I'm still here, still with you, my friends, still out here on the far frontier of freedom, doing battle nightly against the entrenched forces of liberalism, of Big Brother government, of those 'activists' who want to impose their regulations, their busybodyism, on you, tell you how to live your life, take your hard-earned tax dollars to support somebody else's lifestyle."

In the control room, K. T. Zorn shook her head. Not her politics. But she had to admire him. Jerry Knight knew how to grab an audience.

Sammy, the Vietnamese technician, was monitoring his dials closely. When Jerry was on a tear, the volume needle bounced up into the red if he didn't watch it.

K.T. looked at her console. All fifteen incoming phone lines were already flashing and he hadn't been on the air five minutes. Jerry was stirring up the animals. It was going to be wild tonight.

"Nobody's going to shut me up, friends. No way. The Night Talker is going to keep on telling the truth to America, deflating the windbags of Washington, exposing the bull. I am indestructible! I am the voice of truth and justice!

"Now, fortunately, I was not in the car when it blew up. My ex-wife Lila was in the car when it blew up. You've heard me talk about Lila before, so you know how relieved I am, how very, very relieved I am that she suffered only minor injuries."

His voice was thick with irony.

K.T. imagined all those men out there cackling at Jerry's wit.

"Now, I know you're wondering whether the police have caught the miscreant who tried to blow up Jerry Knight," the host told his listeners.

"Well, of course they haven't. Not a clue. You know what I think of the ability of our law-enforcement agencies to get the criminals off the streets. But wait! There may be hope after all. Not long ago, as you remember, a guest on this program was brutally murdered, beaten to death right out-side this studio, in the parking garage, on a main street of your nation's capital. Well, the police have just arrested the man they say did it. Some poor homeless guy who should have been in an institution somewhere, getting the care he needs. But, of course, the liberals of this country let all the mental cases out of the institutions a few years back . . ."

And so on until the first commercial break.

CHAPTER FORTY-THREE

AFTER THE COMMERCIAL, Jerry introduced his guest, a second-string Hollywood actor booked by a PR agency to talk about his new movie.

It was a no-brainer for Jerry to wisecrack his way through the interview. The star wanted to talk about himself. The host insisted on asking him about the liberal "Kulture Korps" in Hollywood.

At two A.M. the star departed. Jerry opened the phones for three hours of Talk Back, America. And, as K.T. had anticipated, it was wild.

The very first caller snarled into the phone, "I'm sorry they got Lila instead of you. Next time, mother—"

Sammy hit the censor switch before the full obscenity could go out over the air.

The second caller announced, "Hey, Jerry, listen. I love you, man. I got an M-16 I brought back from Nam. Know what I mean? You give the word, buddy, I'm up there in D.C.

in a minute. Know what I mean? I'll be your bodyguard, Jerry. Nobody's going to fool with the Night Talker with me around, man. And that includes the cops. Know what I mean, buddy?"

And it was downhill from there.

Coming out of the five-minute break for news at four A.M., K.T. instructed Jerry via the computer screen in front of him to pick up the caller on line twelve.

"Sounds strange," she typed.

Don't they all, Jerry thought.

The host punched up line twelve.

"Jerry? Jerry Knight? Is that you?"

"It is I. The one and only Night Talker, in person. What can I do for you?"

"Am I on the air?"

"Yes, you are. Go ahead."

"I know why Curtis Davenport was killed."

"Yeah?"

Jerry had talked to plenty of irrational callers over the years. This guy sounded agitated but rational.

"Davenport was killed because he was going to blow the whistle on a big scandal on the Hill."

"The Jacobsen thing," Jerry responded.

"No. He knew about Jacobsen. But that wasn't it. It was something else, something bigger. He was going to go public with it. They killed him to stop him."

"What do you mean 'something bigger'?" Who's 'they'? The cops arrested somebody they say did it. A homeless guy."

"I don't want to say any more. I shouldn't have called."

"No, wait! Don't hang up!"

There was a click on the line, and then a dial tone.

Jerry signaled K.T. to trace the call. She nodded.

Meanwhile, there was nothing he could do until he'd bantered through a final hour of Talk Back, America. As soon as the last notes of the closing theme music faded away, he rushed to the control room.

K.T. held out a strip of computer paper.

Jerry took it.

It read: *Guy C. Drummond, 14572 Hunting Farm Creek Court, Gaithersburg, Md. 20879. 301–555–2450.*

Jerry pulled K.T. to him and hugged her. Her close-cropped hair came to the middle of his chest.

"He sounded like he really knows something."

"I *told* you to take the call," K.T. said.

"K.T., you are a genius."

"This comes as big news to you?"

CHAPTER FORTY-FOUR

Jerry had wanted to phone Jane Day as soon as he got off the air, but decided she might not appreciate a call at five A.M. He'd better wait.

It was Saturday, Jerry's day to get up at noon and keep normal people's hours for two days. As soon as his alarm woke him, he phoned Jane at home.

"It's the world's greatest living talk-show host, with very big news," he announced when she answered.

"I could have sworn I turned my radio off."

"I'm coming to you live!"

"What is it, Jerry? I'm on my way out the door."

"Did you hear the show last night?"

"Jerry, you're funny sometimes. And you're not *quite* as big a jerk as I first thought you were. But me, listen to your show? Don't press your luck."

Jerry told her about the mystery caller and what he'd

said about Davenport's death. He invited her to come with him to visit Guy Drummond.

"When?"

"Right now."

"How do you know he's home?"

"I don't. I want to drop in on him unexpectedly. I don't think he'd *be* home if I told him we're coming."

"What's Detective Jones say about this? He thinks he's got the killer."

"I haven't told Jones about Drummond. Like you say, he thinks he's got his killer. He can claim he's closed the case. He's not going to be interested in checking out Drummond's story."

"Why do you want me to go with you?" she asked. She thought she knew the answer.

"I like your company."

Yep. She knew the answer.

"I'll go with you as the *Washington Post* reporter covering the Davenport murder. Nothing else."

"What else could I possibly have on my mind?"

Jane let the question pass.

"I've got to go out and buy cat food. I'll be back in a half hour. Pick me up then."

After she hung up, Jane thought momentarily about calling Drummond and getting the story herself.

Nah. That would be wrong.

CHAPTER FORTY-FIVE

JERRY PICKED UP Jane forty-five minutes later. She was wearing white jeans with white espadrilles, that pretty rose silk blouse that her mother had sent her for Valentine's Day, and her all-purpose wheat tweed jacket. Briefly she considered an Annie Hall hat to hide the reddish-orange tangle of hair beneath it, but decided that was too unbusinesslike. This was, after all, an interview, not a date. She'd have to make that clear to Jerry, who seemed to think any woman, even a liberal, was susceptible to his charms.

"How'd you trace Drummond, anyhow?" Jane asked as soon as she got into the car Jerry had rented to replace his bombed Cadillac.

"And a good morning to you, too," Jerry answered, thinking how single-minded she was about her work.

"Do your phones have caller ID?" she asked, oblivious to his retort.

"Yeah, they do," Jerry replied. "It's for the benefit of the sales department. The system captures the numbers of every-one who calls the show, runs them through a computer data base that looks up the names, addresses, and zip codes, and prints out the whole list. The sales department uses the information to calculate the demographics of our audience for sponsors."

"I'd guess the demographics of your audience are over-weight divorced blue-collar white guys, thirty-five to fifty-five years old, who eat pizza out of the box, belong to the National Rifle Association, and have an IQ in the double dig-its."

"Very funny." Maybe her attitude toward him wasn't softening after all, he thought.

"Can you really get a demographic profile from tracing the calls?" Jane asked.

"Sure. They sell the lists to catalog companies and tele-marketers."

"Two million Jerry Knight fans! Companies must be dying to get a hold of those customers. I bet the lists are real hot with fishing-worm suppliers and phone-sex services."

"Did you ever consider that your view of me and my audience may be a cliché?"

"Sometimes clichés are true," she declared.

Interstate 270 sliced northwest from the Washington Beltway through a string of Maryland suburbs: Bethesda, Rockville, Gaithersburg, Germantown, and Frederick.

"You know this highway was built in the 1950s, as an evacuation route to allow government workers to escape in case a nuclear war seemed imminent," Jane offered.

"Well, it's still an escape route, isn't it?" Jerry respond-ed. "It allows commuters and companies to escape from the problems of downtown Washington."

They drove through land that only a few years before

had been cornfields and grazing pastures for cattle. Now it was a swath of subdivisions, town house developments, and office parks.

Guy Drummond lived off the Shady Grove interchange in a cluster of one hundred town houses. A weather-beaten sign at the entrance pretentiously identified the development as THE HOMES AT HUNTING FARM CREEK.

They looked shabby.

The pastel clapboard was fading and streaked. Here and there an aluminum window screen hung askew. The tiny grass plots were scarred with bare patches.

Jerry parked his car hood-first in a lined-off space around the corner from Drummond's town house. He didn't want Drummond to see them approaching.

A stout man in his mid- or late fifties answered the door.

"Yes?"

"Guy Drummond?"

"Yes. What is—" He looked past Jane. "Oh, my God! You're Jerry Knight, aren't you? Oh, my God. How'd you find me?"

"May we come in?"

Drummond, confused by the unexpected visitors, didn't object.

Jane sized up the place. The furniture was nondescript maple colonial with fading plaid upholstery, cheap and worn. Dirty dishes in the sink and on the countertop in the kitchen. An overflowing ashtray on the coffee table.

The place was dark and depressing.

No woman lives here, Jane concluded, although there were photos of two women in silver frames on the mantel, one middle-aged, staring prim and unsmiling into the camera, the other a younger woman astride a horse.

"You shouldn't have come," Drummond protested, recovering from his initial surprise. "If I'd known you were going to find me, I'd never have called. I can be in big trouble."

He looked questioningly at Jane.

"I'm Jane Day." She stuck out her hand, but didn't reveal she was a reporter.

"Jane Day? Aren't you the one who wrote the Jacobsen story in the *Post*?"

She nodded.

"Oh, no! This is even worse."

Jerry sat down in a plaid armchair. Jane sat on the sofa. It smelled dusty.

Drummond retrieved a pack of unfiltered Camels from the mantel, lit up, and sat down at the other end of the sofa, exhaling a cloud of smoke with a resigned sigh.

"Why'd you come?"

"You said on the phone last night that Davenport was killed so he wouldn't expose a scandal, something bigger than the Jacobsen case," Jerry replied. "We want to know more."

"I never should have called."

"Tell us what you know," Jerry urged.

"I can't," Drummond said, puffing nervously on his cigarette. "I'm sorry. I can't."

Jane studied him. He looked familiar. There were so many like him in Washington, aging, portly, faceless bureaucrats who had worked behind the scenes too long, producing ideas for which others got credit, paying deference for too long to politicians they don't respect, keeping their head down, waiting for retirement.

"You work on the Hill, don't you?" Jane guessed. It was a long shot.

And accurate. Drummond's resistance weakened.

"Yes," he conceded. "I work for Jacobsen. And if he finds out I'm talking to you, I'll be fired."

Jane thought she remembered him now, sitting in the staff seats at subcommittee hearings.

Jerry decided he was going to have to use his interview skills if they were to get any useful information out of Drummond.

Strategy number one: sympathize.

"You sound like you're not too happy working for Jacobsen," he prodded.

"I'm not too happy with any of them anymore," Drummond replied, his defenses crumbling. "When I came to the Hill, there were giants up there. Hubert Humphrey, Barry Goldwater, Scoop Jackson. Claude Pepper was still alive. Men of character, men who believed in something, who fought for what they believed in, but without destroying the people on the other side. They could disagree without being disagreeable. Look at what you've got now. This bunch doesn't stand for anything, except getting themselves on TV or in the newspaper by cutting up the opposition. They won't vote for anything they think will make anybody mad. So nothing gets done. Running for reelection has become their full-time occupation. Or, I should say, raising money to run for reelection is their full-time occupation. The PAC's give them money. The special interests give them money. And that money buys access and influence the average ordinary person doesn't have. That was a good story you wrote, Miss Day. But you didn't even scratch the surface of what's going on. I hate what Congress has become. When I first came here, I felt like I was going to help fix what was wrong with our country. But now . . . That's why I like your show, Jerry. You know the system's rotten. And you say so."

Jerry dipped his head, acknowledging the compliment.

"Why don't you retire?" Jane asked.

"I thought of it when Grace died," Drummond responded, nodding toward the photo of the older woman on the mantel. "But I can't afford to. Grace's illness cost . . . and my daughter is in medical school. I'm helping her."

He nodded toward the other photo. Drummond crushed out his cigarette in the overflowing ashtray. Suddenly, his caution returned.

"Look, I can't talk to you anymore." He looked back and forth between Jane and Jerry. "If Jacobsen finds out I'm talking to you like this, I'll be fired. I can't afford to lose my job at this time in my life."

"You won't be fired if nobody knows you're talking to us," Jane assured him. "And nobody will know."

"I'm sorry. I can't."

"I was a friend of Curtis Davenport's," Jane told him with all the sincerity she could put into it. "I want to know who killed him. I want that person caught and punished. Please help."

"I was a friend of Curtis's, too," Drummond replied. "I'm the one who told him about Jacobsen and Z-Chem."

A light bulb went off in Jane's head. Guy Drummond was the source. She'd assumed all along that Jennifer Hurst had leaked the Z-Chem story to Curtis. But it had been Drummond. He must be very bitter if he was willing to blow the whistle on the senator he worked for.

"You said on the phone last night that Davenport was getting ready to spill an even bigger scandal," Jerry prodded.

Drummond lit another Camel and inhaled it deeply. He studied the pictures of his wife and daughter. The only sound in the dim room was from the children playing outside.

"You've got to protect me," Drummond said. "My name can never be connected to this in any way."

"Absolutely," Jane assured him.

"Promise?"

"Yes," Jane and Jerry said in unison.

Looking scared and unhappy, Drummond told his story.

"I first met Davenport more than ten years ago. I'd been a staffer for a long time and he was a novice environmental lobbyist. We shared the same outlook on issues and the same belief that rational, progressive legislation would gradually make America a better place. We also shared a cynicism that members of Congress were more interested in getting reelected than they were in passing progressive legislation.

"We often had lunch or drinks together. Once Davenport tipped me that the environmentalists would be willing to lengthen the time companies had to comply with toxic waste clean-up regulations in exchange for more stringent restrictions in the future. I passed the information to Jacobsen, who wrote the compromise into a pending bill.

"When I learned that Jacobsen had received a campaign 'loan' from Z-Chem after interceding with the EPA, I griped about it to Davenport over beers one night at the Hawk 'n' Dove. I'd complained to him before about things I'd seen on the Hill. I knew he leaked them to the press. But my name was never connected. I trusted him.

"He obviously told you about Jacobsen," Drummond concluded, nodding at Jane. "You want to hear the sickest part of all? I'm the one who was assigned to draft the statement Jacobsen read at his news conference denying it! They've infected me. I've become as big a hypocrite as the rest of them."

"You said when you called the *Night Talker* show that Curtis was killed to stop him from revealing an even bigger scandal," Jane prodded gently.

"You swear you'll never reveal my name?" Drummond demanded again. "I'd be fired in a minute."

"Please, trust us," Jane said.

"I guess I have to. I guess I want the world to know."

"Do it for Curtis," Jane encouraged him. "Help us find out who killed him."

"The cops never will," Jerry chimed in.

Drummond puffed his cigarette.

"The evening Curtis went on your program, I learned something new about Z-Chem. I phoned him at the studio to tell him about it. It seems—"

"It was *you* who called him?" Jerry cut in. "But the number you left was Jack VanDyke's office."

"That's right. I work out of VanDyke's suite of offices. It's the same extension."

The mention of VanDyke distracted Drummond from his story.

"I hate Jack VanDyke," he spat. "He's the symbol of everything that's wrong with politics today. He'd kill his own grandmother if he—"

Drummond stopped abruptly, realizing what he'd said.

"Would he?" Jerry asked.

"I don't know," Drummond replied.

"Did you call Curtis to tell him something about VanDyke?" Jane asked.

"No. I called to tell him I'd learned that Drake Dennis was somehow involved in a deal with Z-Chem. Drake Dennis. He *pretends* to be an environmental activist."

"I *knew* he was a fake!" Jerry said. "Drake the Fake. I

always called him that. And I was right! I should have run him over the other night when he staged one of his demonstrations on Memorial Bridge."

"What kind of 'deal'?" Jane asked.

"I'm not sure," Drummond replied. "It was something I overheard. I didn't get the details. It was some kind of under-the-table deal between Z-Chem and Dennis. And they didn't want anybody to know about it."

"So, when you called Jerry's show last night, you were suggesting that Drake Dennis killed Curtis to prevent him from revealing this 'deal'?" Jane asked.

"I don't know. I don't know." Drummond was growing agitated, rocking back and forth, his hands clenched across his belly. "I've told you everything I know. You have to go now. Please. I never should have called the show. But I've told you everything and you've got to leave. Please leave now!"

Jerry and Jane looked at each other. Drummond seemed to be on the verge of falling apart.

At the door, Drummond demanded assurance anew that his identity would never be revealed. They again promised to keep his name out of it.

At the last instant, he said, "I want the system to change. Maybe it will change, if you tell about this."

CHAPTER FORTY-SIX

JANE AND JERRY didn't see the car tailing them out of the town house development and south again on I-270. They had no reason to notice.

They were busy talking about what Drummond had just told them.

Jerry beseeched Jane to join him for a late lunch on the outdoor terrace at Angler's Inn, perfect for a warm spring Saturday.

Jane resisted, but weakly.

"You've got to eat *somewhere*," Jerry argued convincingly.

She couldn't think of a comeback. It seemed that without any spoken agreement, they had become informal partners in a murder investigation.

But not friends.

At the end of the interstate, Jerry continued south on the Beltway. He exited at River Road, cut over to MacArthur Boulevard, and headed west on the twisting two-lane road.

The other car followed at each turn.

Angler's was a squat green-awninged country house, stone on the ground floor, cream-colored stucco and timbers on the second, surrounded by stone terraces and fountains, gardens and ancient trees. The place attracted an eclectic clientele, ranging from tourists to ambassadors, and the estated gentry of nearby Potomac to hikers and bicyclists off the C & O Canal trail just across the road.

The tuxedoed maître d' knew Jerry well, and escorted them to a good table, under a green and white umbrella, in an uncrowded part of the terrace next to a fountain.

"This place is one of the things I like best about Washington," Jerry said. "Did you know Angler's opened the same year the Civil War started?"

"No, but I've heard the gossip about Angler's," Jane said. "I hear that a lot of well-known men in Washington like to bring their girlfriends here because they're not likely to bump into their wives."

"I wouldn't know about that." Jerry grinned.

"Can I help you?" the maître d' asked the man who had trailed Jerry and Jane from Gaithersburg. The man brushed past. His coat was open, and the maître d' saw a gun.

"Hey!"

Before the maître d' could sound a warning, the man was at their table.

"Detective Jones!" Jerry exclaimed. "What are you doing here?"

The flustered maître d' rushed up.

"There'll be three for lunch," the detective told him. Jones pulled over a white plastic chair from an adjacent table and sat down.

The maître d' hurried away for an extra place setting.

"So, we've got the Jerry and Jane Private Detective Agency here, ain't we."

"What's that supposed to mean?" Jerry asked.

"Cut the crap, okay? I was on a stakeout last night, trying to nail a girl stabbed her boyfriend. I listened to your program in the car while I was waiting for her to show up at her mama's house. Heard that guy called in, said he knew the real reason Davenport was busted. I figured you and the *Washington Post* here were so interested in the case, you would try to find out what that was all about. So I followed you. Over to Adams-Morgan to pick her up, out to Gaithersburg, back down here to—"

"The police have no right to follow innocent people!" Jane protested.

"Hi, I'm Philip, and I'll be your server today," the waiter announced chirpily. "Would anyone care for a drink while you're looking at the menus?"

Jane ordered an iced tea and the others followed suit.

Philip departed. Jones bent over the white tablecloth and spoke to Jerry and Jane in a deep, intense rumble.

"Listen, man. I told you before, this ain't no damn game. I got a captain on my back giving me a lot of heat to nail the one popped Davenport."

"I thought you arrested some homeless guy for that," Jerry chided. "Are you admitting you got the wrong man?"

"Man, you are unbelievable," the detective complained.

"Leave us alone," Jane said angrily. "You're not even supposed to be out here. You're D.C. police and this is Maryland."

Philip appeared.

"Iced teas here?" He distributed the glasses. "Our specials today are—"

"Later." Jones looked at the waiter menacingly.

"Just let me know when you're ready," Philip said, and sauntered away.

Jones sucked in a deep breath and made an appeal for their help.

"The police are a bunch of sorry asses sometimes. And we've got more murders than we can handle in this city. But we've got resources you ain't got. Maybe you've got the resources to nail some politician with his hand in the cookie jar. But you ain't got the resources to catch who popped Davenport. You can't catch 'em but maybe I can. But I need your damn help."

People at other tables were looking at them.

"Maybe that homeless guy did pop Davenport," Jones continued. "But maybe he didn't. There's a lot of puzzle pieces left over that don't fit that picture."

A.L. paused for a gulp of iced tea.

"Miss Washington Post, you want to know who did your friend. And you also want a story. Mr. Night Talker, you want bad guys off the street. Okay, you tell me what you know, we'll make all that happen."

"Ready to order?"

Philip was back.

They all ordered the grilled swordfish to get rid of him.

Jones took one last shot at persuading them to cooperate.

"You hear things. People talk to you who won't talk to me. I hear things. I talk to people who won't talk to you. You got part of the puzzle. I got part of the puzzle. You tell me what you know, we got the whole puzzle figured out, we catch the mother. You don't tell me what you know, the mother's gonna walk free."

"If I help you and you do catch him, will you come on my show as a guest?" Jerry bargained.

"How about *me*?" Jane jumped in. "If I tell you what I

know, will you give me a break when you catch him? Tell me before you announce it to the other reporters?"

A.L. nodded his agreement to their terms.

Jerry and Jane looked at each other.

"All right," Jerry acceded.

For the next hour they sat in the milky spring sunshine on the almost empty terrace, ate swordfish, drank iced tea, and exchanged information.

First, Jerry told about their conversation with Guy Drummond, including his last phone call to Davenport about some kind of under-the-table deal between Z-Chem and Drake Dennis, the environmental guerrilla. Jones agreed not to interrogate Drummond unless he had to. He'd try to get Dennis to talk.

Jane provided more details of Curtis's threat at Bull Feathers to expose Capitol drug dealers, and of Jennifer Hurst's confidences. She rationalized her betrayal of a source by telling herself that Jones could find out on his own.

Jones asked a lot of questions about the drug angle, in the process revealing his visit with Frog in the Anacostia cemetery, and his interrogation of Pat Howell on suspicion of running cocaine on the Hill.

Jerry and Jane were stunned by that information.

Jerry divulged his strange encounter at the J. W. Marriott with the drunken Kurt Voss, and how Voss had expressed pleasure at Davenport's death.

Voss? Jones remembered the name. He flipped through his bent notebook. There. Kurt Voss. Pat Howell's boyfriend. Her alibi for the time of Davenport's murder. She'd said they'd been in bed together at that moment.

"Who's Kurt Voss?" the detective asked.

"A lobbyist," Jane answered. "And one of his clients is Z-Chem."

"Which is?" Jones looked puzzled.

"The company I wrote about. They gave Senator Jacobsen a hundred-thousand-dollar payoff to fix a problem with the EPA."

"And the company that had some kind of deal with Drake Dennis too, according to Drummond," Jerry added.

"Curtis was my source for the Jacobsen story," Jane confided. She voiced her concern that if Jacobsen had somehow found out Curtis was the source, the senator, or more likely his henchman VanDyke, might have had Davenport killed in retaliation.

Finally, there was no more information to disclose. They fell silent, picking at the remnants of their swordfish.

They agreed to leave the heavy lifting to Jones. He would question Voss, VanDyke, and Dennis, after first advising the captain that some big-time toes were about to get stepped on. Jerry would try to draw additional information from Pat Howell. And Jane would meet again with Jennifer Hurst.

A.L.'s walkie-talkie crackled.

"Yeah?"

He listened to the static.

"I got to go," he informed them, rising from the table. "Drive-by in the Greenway neighborhood."

He reached for his wallet to pay his share of the check. Jerry waved the money away.

Jones shambled across the terrace, got into his white car, and drove from the idyllic Maryland countryside to the war zone of Washington's Greenway neighborhood.

What a difference twenty miles makes.

CHAPTER FORTY-SEVEN

JERRY AND JANE lingered at the table a few more minutes after Jones's departure, finishing their coffee, tugging at the skein of connections the lunch had revealed.

They meandered through the gardens on the way to his rented car. Jane dropped a quarter into a wooden wishing well. She silently wished for better hair and ten fewer pounds.

When they drove back inside the city limits, MacArthur Boulevard had the appearance of a quiet, tree-shaded boulevard in a medium-sized city, rather than a main thoroughfare of a world capital. A grass strip down the middle of the street was planted with flower beds cultivated by the residents. The houses were a jumble of styles, ages, and price ranges. They were interspersed with neighborhood cafes, delis, and dry cleaners.

As they drove, Jerry asked Jane if she was interested in seeing a movie.

"No, thanks," she replied.

"Why not?"

"I have a date," she lied. Well, it wasn't completely a lie. She had a date with Bloomsbury.

But the real reason she said no was that after spending a Saturday afternoon with this man, she needed to figure out what she really thought of him.

"I'm sorry," Jerry said.

"Sorry I have a date?"

"Sorry it isn't me."

She swallowed a devastating put-down line before it popped out.

CHAPTER FORTY-EIGHT

JERRY HATED SATURDAY nights.

The radio show was the center of his life. On the nights he didn't have to go to the studio, he felt adrift and lonely.

Keyed up from the trip to Gaithersburg and the lunch at Angler's, he prowled his apartment forlornly. He considered his options.

The Orioles were on a road trip, so there was no baseball. The Palm would be filled with tourists wearing the wrong clothes. They'd spot him and come to his table for his autograph and his opinions. He couldn't stand that.

Rent a movie and order pizza delivered? See what's on cable? Read?

Jerry didn't feel like spending the night alone.

He thought of K.T. She wouldn't have a date. He'd have dinner with her. Tell her about his day.

"What are you doing?" Jerry asked when K.T. picked up the phone.

"What are you doing, taking a survey? It's Saturday, isn't it? Last time I looked at my contract, I'm not required to report what I do on my own time."

"I thought you might want to have dinner."

They're all the same, K.T. thought. Lost little boys when cut off from their adoring audience. Donahue had been like that. Always calling her for company whenever Marlo was out of town.

"I'm with my friend," K.T. informed Jerry.

"Bring her along."

"She doesn't like you."

"She doesn't like men."

"Smart."

"I went out and talked to Drummond today. I've got a lot to tell you. Over dinner."

"Wait a minute."

K.T. covered the mouthpiece with her hand. Jerry couldn't make out the muffled conversation at the other end of the line.

"Kim's got to go into her office for a couple of hours," K.T. reported when she came back on the phone. "I'll meet you for dinner. It'll be my good deed for the week."

Jerry ignored the jibe, grateful for her companionship.

"Where do you want to meet?" he asked.

"Annie's Steak House. Seventeenth and R."

"That's . . ."—he stopped himself before he called it a gay hangout—"fine."

Annie's was in a funky neighborhood east of Dupont Circle on the fringe of downtown. The restaurant stood out on the block because of a spacious glassed-in dining room encroaching on the sidewalk. Jerry hoped K.T. hadn't chosen a table there. If he sat on the black leatherette banquette facing in, he'd be spotted by a roomful of diners. If he sat in one of the curved-back armchairs facing out, he'd be spotted by people passing by on the street. He didn't need anyone spreading rumors that he was gay.

He didn't have to worry. He found K.T. in a dark booth inside the bar. Jerry sat facing away from the crowd.

"So, what's Drummond's story?" K.T. asked after the waitress in black jeans and white cotton blouse had delivered their drinks. Cherry daiquiri for her. The usual gin martini and onion for him.

Jerry recounted the story of the visit to Gaithersburg and the addition of Drake Dennis to the list of suspects. He told her about Jones accosting him and Jane Day at Angler's and badgering them for information on Davenport's murder. He enumerated the suspects who popped up as they exchanged information. And he related that in return for sharing what he knew, he had extracted a promise from the detective to appear as a guest on the *Night Talker* show if he caught the killer.

"You think he'll catch him?" K.T. asked.

"No."

K.T. rubbed the rim of her daiquiri glass back and forth over her upper lip and gazed into the distance, hatching an idea. Jerry drained his martini.

When the waitress came back, K.T. ordered one of the surf-and-turf combinations, steak and shrimp, a specialty at Annie's. Jerry settled for a chicken and Monterey Jack cheese sandwich, and another martini.

"I've got an idea," K.T. offered.

"Yeah?"

"You ever read those British mystery novels, where the detective gathers all the suspects into the drawing room of a big country house and tricks the murderer into confessing?"

"I guess I've read a couple like that. What's that got to do—"

"We do a modern version. We invite all the suspects in Davenport's murder to appear on the *Night Talker* show. The pretext would be a roundtable discussion on environmental issues—no, wait, we're staging a National Town Meeting. That's the hot thing these days. And during the show, you trick the murderer into confessing."

"That's all I have to do?"

"If you don't think you can handle it . . ."

"I can handle it." The idea was growing on him.

"The ratings would go through the roof," K.T. elaborated. "C-SPAN might cover it live. And the publicity would blow Rush Limbaugh away."

"How can you be sure the suspects would come?" Jerry asked.

"You give free airtime, they'll come," K.T. said disdainfully. "In Washington, media exposure is the opiate of the asses."

"K.T., you have a way with words."

"Thank you."

He worked on his second martini and considered her plan. The environmental Town Meeting idea was a good cover story. All the suspects had at least a vague involvement with the issue. Drake Dennis, of course Jack VanDyke, because of the Z-Chem case. Maybe Senator Jacobsen for the same reason although Jerry still resisted the idea that such a staunch conservative could be involved. Pat Howell, who did PR for clients with environmental problems, Kurt Voss, Z-Chem's lobbyist. It might be plausible enough to get them into the studio.

Of course, maybe the murderer wasn't on their list. Maybe it really was that homeless guy the cops already had in custody. Still, as K.T. said, great for ratings, great for publicity.

"Let's do it," he decided. "We've come up with a great idea."

"What's that 'we' shit?" K.T. replied.

CHAPTER FORTY-NINE

A S IT TURNED out, not much progress was made over the next few days on the assignments outlined at Angler's.

Pat Howell was too busy to have lunch with Jerry. Jennifer Hurst was out of town. And A. L. Jones had no time to interview suspects because he was working twenty hours a day on a gang war that had broken out between two crews in the Greenway neighborhood.

Jones was driving back to Homicide at three o'clock one morning when he heard the promotional announcement for the Environmental Town Meeting coming up on Friday on the *Night Talker* show. When he heard the names of the participants, the detective knew exactly what Jerry was up to.

"You stupid white man," A.L. shouted at his car radio.

At five A.M., Jones phoned Jerry and tried to talk him out of the Town Meeting.

"You're trying to get one of 'em to confess on the air, ain't you?"

"Sure," Jerry acknowledged. "Why not? The investigation is going nowhere. I figure it can't hurt."

"Suppose it ain't one of them four?" A.L. argued. "Suppose it's the street bum we arrested?"

"Do you really believe he killed Davenport?"

"Could have," the detective replied unconvincingly.

"You pin it on him before Friday, we'll dump the Town Meeting and put you on to tell how you did it. Make you a hero."

"Man, you don't know what you're getting into. If it was a drug thing, you don't want to be messing with it. Somebody already blowed up your car."

"Tune in Friday," Jerry told him. "Should be exciting."

An hour later, Jerry was finishing off his second beer, preparing to sleep, when the phone in his apartment rang.

"Damn you!" the voice on the phone screeched.

"Lila?"

"It's not Lila! It's Jane Day!"

"Why did the front desk put you through?" Jerry mumbled. "It's my sleeping time."

"I told them it was the White House calling."

"You professional journalists have your little tricks, don't you? What's up? I'm getting ready for bed."

"I just saw the ad in the paper for your Friday-night show," Jane said angrily. "Very clever. Invite all the suspects in Curtis's murder, expose the killer, get a ton of publicity. That's it, isn't it?"

Jerry plumped up the pillows behind him. It sounded like he was going to be on the phone a while.

"So? Don't you want Davenport's killer exposed?"

"This is *my* story. *I* want to break it. I *need* it."

"Isn't that just a tad on the selfish side?"

"As opposed to your altruistic reasons? Like ratings? Like publicity? Like your gigantic macho ego?"

"The show isn't until Friday night. That gives you almost four days to solve the murder, break the story, win yourself a Pulitzer. Be my guest."

"You know half the suspects won't even talk to me," Jane said.

"And why is that?" Jerry said, savoring her acknowledgement. "Because they know that liberal rag you work for is likely to do a hatchet job on them?"

"No! Because I'm a local reporter, not a big-foot national reporter. And because the paper caved to Jacobsen and left me hanging out to dry."

"So if you break the story, you redeem your reputation, move to the national desk, and become the female Bob Woodward. Right?"

"Why do you put such a negative spin on everything? Curtis was my friend. I want to know who killed him."

Jerry let his eyes droop shut and listened to her heavy breathing on the other end of the line.

"Okay, listen. I'm sorry. I understand your feelings. How's this? The suspects won't talk to you, but they will talk to me. So, Friday night why don't you come on the show, as the guest cohost. You've covered environmental issues, so it'll seem legitimate. As soon as the murderer reveals himself, you call the paper with the story."

"The first edition is out at nine-thirty. Your show doesn't go on the air until midnight. You'll scoop me."

"You'll make the final edition. You'll have the story. And you'll have your friend's murderer."

Again, he listened to her breathing.

"It's the best deal you're going to get," he prodded. "Take it."

"Jerry, you're an asshole," she said.

"I'm going to assume that's not intended as a compliment."

CHAPTER FIFTY

TWO O'CLOCK THE next morning.

A cruiser patrol had caught a thirteen-year-old boy breaking into a record store. He was carrying a nine-millimeter and he bragged about being one of the shooters in the Greenway gang war.

A. L. Jones questioned the boy, then took him to a D.C. juvenile detention center. Like many of the young detainees, he would probably escape.

Driving back to the Homicide office, Jones listened to the *Night Talker* show. Promos for the Friday-night Town Meeting rekindled his anger. He cursed the white mother.

Back in the office, the detective sat at his desk and stared at the jumble of untended paperwork. He drank lukewarm bitter coffee from a paper cup.

He felt old, tired, and helpless.

Jones flipped on his computer. It flickered on, went off,

flickered on again, displaying a jumble of meaningless letters.

Sometimes the damn thing worked, sometimes it didn't.

He slapped the side of the monitor with his flat palm and the screen cleared.

The detective consulted his notebook. He tore off a piece of a white 7-Eleven bag in the wastebasket and wrote on it the names of the suspects in the Davenport killing.

Kurt Voss. Patricia Howell. Drake Dennis. Jack VanDyke. Jacobsen. Kruk, the homeless guy.

Using the computer, he searched for information about each name that might help pinpoint which, if any, had busted Davenport.

After an hour, he pushed back from the computer. His stubby fingers were beginning to hit too many wrong keys. He poured himself another cup of coffee and mindlessly watched an old movie on the TV for a while. Then he returned to the screen.

After another hour, he'd put the puzzle pieces together in a way that made a picture. There were some pieces left over. And there were some blank places in the picture.

But he thought he knew who had popped Davenport.

He stood up and put his coat on. Five in the morning. Time to go home.

"Hey, A.L. Come on, ride with me, man." It was Chapin, another Homicide detective.

"Old lady busted in her house over near that Jewish graveyard in Anacostia. My eyes tell me your friend Frog's crew might of been the shooters."

No. Not her. Please, God. Not her.

CHAPTER FIFTY-ONE

JERRY WAS UNCHARACTERISTICALLY nervous before the Friday-night show.

Jane was uncharacteristically calm. One of her fantasies was to be a regular panelist on a Washington talking-head TV show. This was a start.

K.T. was efficient, as always, hunched over her omnipresent clipboard.

Sammy, the Vietnamese engineer, grinned behind his control board. He had more microphone checks to run than he'd ever had before. Six people were crowded around the baize-covered table in the studio.

Only Jacobsen had declined the invitation to appear on the program. Dennis, Howell, Voss, and VanDyke had accepted. Even though only Dennis could rightly be called an environmental expert, for the others the lure of a national radio network audience in the millions had been irresistible, as K.T. had predicted.

If any suspected the National Town Meeting was a setup to squeeze a confession out of one of them live on the air, none showed it.

In fact, K.T. had been bombarded with calls from environmental activists, trade associations, and major polluters demanding to be included on the panel. She had assured them they would be considered for a later show.

As the studio clock ticked down to midnight, Voss, VanDyke, and Howell traded inconsequential small talk. Drake Dennis rummaged inside the green backpack stuffed under his chair. Jane studied her notes. Jerry stared at his reflection in the glass wall separating the studio from the control room. He sipped tea from a mug, and hummed up and down the scale to warm up his vocal cords.

Midnight.

The theme music blared from the speakers, then faded.

"It's midnight and ATN, the All Talk Network, presents radio's most popular all-night talkmeister, Jerry Knight, and the *Night Talker* show, live from Washington, D.C. If you're working, studying, or just having trouble sleeping, you are not alone. Tonight, Jerry presents a special program, a National Town Meeting on environmental issues, featuring a panel of experts and his guest cohost, Jane Day of the *Washington Post*. For the next five hours, sit back and listen while Jerry entertains, informs, and sometimes enrages you. Ladies and gentlemen, here to keep you company all night is Jerry Knight, the Night Talker!"

The theme music swelled. The red ON AIR light flashed. Sammy jabbed his finger at Jerry.

"Yes! Yes! I am here among you yet again, the world's certified greatest living talk-show host. And since Superman is dead, I am here representing the last bastion of truth, justice, and the American way."

K.T. looked up from her clipboard. Was that a quaver in Jerry's voice? Could the world's certified greatest living talk-show host be nervous? Sammy glanced at K.T. He'd heard it, too.

"And tonight, an incredible program. The latest in an unbroken string of incredible programs, of course. A special National Town Meeting on the environment. You know how I feel about this issue, friends. The earth has survived—what is it?—five billion years? My question is, can it survive another few years of environmental kookism? To help determine the answer, we have right here with us tonight, live and in person, probably the world's foremost practitioner of environmental kookism, Commander Doom himself."

Jerry motioned toward Drake Dennis as if the radio audience could see him. The host introduced the rest of his guests in kinder terms.

Aware that the clock was ticking toward the deadline for the *Post's* final edition, Jane was anxious to begin. She fidgeted in her chair and twisted a strand of curly orange hair around her finger.

Up to the first commercial break, they stuck to the announced topic of the show, the environment. Drake was outrageous and provocative, as usual. Voss and Howell doggedly defended their clients against his charges. VanDyke, suspecting that Jerry and Jane had some hidden agenda, sat scowling and silent, waiting warily to see what the surprise would be.

After the break, Jane couldn't stand the charade any longer.

"Miss Howell, do you have a side business, something other than your PR agency?" Jane asked.

"I don't know what you mean by a 'side business,' Miss Day," Howell replied sweetly, her Southern accent stretching out "side," turning it into two syllables. "Making sure the public doesn't fall for what you and Mr. Drake say about my clients is a full-time job."

Jane felt awkward, uncertain. This talk-show business was harder than she'd anticipated. She suddenly appreciated what Jerry did night after night.

"So you don't have, like, do another . . . anything else to make money other than PR?" Jane asked inarticulately.

"I certainly do not. I don't know what you're talking about."

The National Town Meeting on the environment was over. The effort to expose Davenport's killer was under way.

Jerry picked up the questioning.

"Mr. Voss, I ran into you a few weeks ago, leaving a reception at the J. W. Marriott. It was shortly after Curtis Davenport was killed following an appearance on this program. Remember that?"

"Uh, vaguely," Voss replied, shifting uneasily in his chair.

"You were pretty drunk."

"That's a lie!"

"At least you'll acknowledge you were pretty angry? Right?"

Voss didn't reply.

"You told me you were glad Davenport had been killed, that you wished you'd done it yourself. Remember that?"

"I certainly do not! I never said such a thing. And I resent you asking me that question. You invited us onto this program for a discussion of environmental issues. Now all of a sudden you start asking me questions about Davenport's murder. Let's get back on the topic."

"I'm the Night Talker," Jerry informed him. "It's my program and I can ask any damn question I want to."

Now VanDyke knew what the surprise was. And Voss,

Howell, and Dennis also had a pretty good idea of what they'd gotten themselves into. But what could they do? Anyone who stalked out would immediately be considered a murder suspect, at least in the eyes of Jerry's two million listeners and the millions more who would hear about it tomorrow. The only alternative was to stay and face Jerry's accusatory questions.

Even the jaded K.T. was enthralled by the on-air drama. For once she put aside her clipboard and watched.

"Mr. Voss, you and Ms. Howell have a close personal relationship, don't you?" Jane asked. "In fact, you live together."

"My personal life is my own business," Pat Howell protested.

Jane ignored her.

"Will you answer my question, Mr. Voss?"

"My relationship with Miss Howell has nothing to do with the announced topic of this program, namely the environment, and I don't intend to talk about it or answer any questions about it," Voss declared.

"Would you be willing to kill to protect your girlfriend?" Jane pursued. "If you thought Curtis was about to blow the whistle on her, to reveal that she was . . . that she was involved in an illegal activity, would you kill to prevent that?"

"This is ridiculous!" Voss shouted.

"This is fantastic!" K.T. exulted in the control room. All fifteen phone lines were flashing with listeners waiting to get in on the questioning. Thousands more must be getting busy signals, the producer guessed.

If the other two guests, Jack VanDyke and Drake Dennis, hoped they were mere props for the interrogation of Voss and Howell, they were now disabused of that idea.

"Speaking of protecting a friend, Jack, did you suspect

that Davenport had fed Miss Day the story about your boss taking a campaign loan from that chemical company? Were you mad enough about it to kill Davenport?" Jerry asked. "After all, that story could destroy Jacobsen's presidential plans."

VanDyke sneered. To him, politics was a full-body contact sport, and the only way to respond to Knight's suggestion was to counterattack.

"You little schmuck. What's the matter? Your ratings going down? So you try to build yourself up by tearing down a great American? Let me tell you something. Somebody who doesn't like the senator dumped a bad story on Jane here and she bit. But it stunk too bad even for the *Post*. The girl reporter here got herself demoted so far down the totem pole she's one step up from covering the zoning board in Dale City. So watch your mouth, Jerry, if you don't want the same thing to happen to you. You keep that motor mouth of yours running, it's going to cost you more money than you and your network have ever seen."

Jerry was aware that he was skirting dangerously close to libel. But from years of interviewing, he knew the program was at a crucial moment. If he backed down or displayed the least bit of concern about VanDyke's threat, he'd lose control of the show. The guests would gain the upper hand and he wouldn't be able to expose Davenport's killer.

The only way to respond to VanDyke's counterattack was to step up the attack.

"Good tirade, Jack. But you didn't answer my questions. So let me try again. Did you suspect Davenport fed Jane that story? Whether the story was true or not, were you mad enough to kill him, or have him killed?"

"You want an answer? The answer is no," VanDyke replied. "Maybe I can be more emphatic. Hell, no."

"I believe what Curtis told me about the hundred thousand dollars from Z-Chem," Jane announced. "And I believe—"

"Ain't that charming?" VanDyke interrupted in a vicious tone. "She bites on a bad story, she gets nailed for it, now she blames a dead man. Nice. Very nice. What kind—"

"I am not blaming—" Jane tried to respond.

"—of people you hanging out with these days, Jerry? I remember when you used to be a conservative. What was it you called yourself? 'A beacon of reason lighting up the dark night of liberalism.' Now look at you. Teaming up with a reporter from the *Washington Post!*"

"We'll be right back after these commercials," Jerry announced into his microphone.

During the break, the atmosphere in the studio was poisonous. VanDyke continued to rage at Jerry for tricking the four of them into this confrontation. Dennis, who hadn't had his turn on the hot seat yet, threatened to direct his supporters to boycott the network and all its advertisers if Jerry suggested on the air that he had anything to do with Davenport's murder. Voss and Howell huddled, whispering.

But none left. Bad as it was to stay, it would be worse to leave.

Jane fairly vibrated with anxiety. She looked at her watch. She was going to miss the final edition if one of them didn't crack soon.

Jerry winked at her. If someone at this table was Davenport's murderer, he was going to find out which one it was.

In the control room, K.T.'s private line buzzed. It was the president of the network demanding to know what the hell was going on.

"Can't talk right now. Too busy."

She'd fight with him in the morning.

The private phone buzzed again. This time it was the Associated Press wanting to know what the hell was going on.

"Keep listening. You'll find out."

The commercials ended, the announcer reintroduced Jerry, and he picked up where he had left off with VanDyke.

"So, Jack, you deny you killed Davenport for leaking the bribe story?"

"Listen, jerk. I was in Chicago the night Davenport was killed, at a fund-raiser with the senator. Hundreds of people saw me there. So, unless you think I was in two places at once, I had nothing to do with Davenport's murder. And if you don't stop suggesting I did, I'm going to sue your ass."

"Maybe you hired someone to do it, Jack," Jerry persisted. "Maybe you got Kurt here to do it. He's a lobbyist for Z-Chem. I know for a fact he was angry at Davenport. He told me—"

"I did not!" Voss interjected.

"But did you get him to do your dirty work?"

"I've said everything I'm going to say. Pick on somebody else."

Jerry did. He turned to Drake Dennis and asked innocently, "You wouldn't have any reason to kill Davenport, would you, Drake? You were both on the same side. You were both of the tree-hugger persuasion."

"Curtis was a wimp," the environmental guerrilla retorted. "Don't put me in the same category with him. Curtis was always talking about 'working within the system' and 'making the law work for the benefit of the people,' and that kind of crap. That approach, begging for crumbs, doesn't work. Only confrontation will stop companies like Z-Chem, represented by Mr. Voss, and the companies represented by Miss Howell, from making planet Earth uninhabitable. Direct action worked at the Boston Tea Party and direct action works today. Only when the people take to the streets in the millions and demand that these companies stop despoiling planet Earth will the environment be saved."

Jerry applauded sarcastically.

"Nice speech, Drake. Probably bring you in a lot of donations."

Dennis ignored him. The environmental activist had the ears of a national audience and he was going to take full advantage of the exposure.

"I'm shocked you would even have Jack VanDyke on a show about the environment, Jerry," Dennis continued. "His boss is probably the worst thing that's happened to the environment since they invented nuclear power. Has Jacobsen ever voted for *any* bill to save planet Earth, Jack?"

"Fortunately for the country," VanDyke responded, "Senator Jacobsen understands that as a national leader, he must balance the all-or-nothing demands of crackpots like you against the needs of workers for jobs and of the economy for growth."

"A 'leader'?" Dennis fired back. "A bribe-taker, you mean. What we don't need in this country is a right-wing President who takes payoffs from polluters to let them keep poisoning our environment. If Jacobsen ever gets to be President, we'll have global warming so bad the North Pole will turn into a beach resort."

The effort to unmask Curtis Davenport's killer had gone off the track. Jerry glanced at Jane, looking for help.

"You sound as if you didn't like Curtis very much, Mr. Dennis," she declared.

"I told you he was a wimp. I disapproved of his methods. But if that were grounds for killing, there'd be a lot of dead lobbyists in Washington."

Dennis cackled wickedly.

Jane was tempted to defend her friend against Dennis's slur. But this wasn't the time.

"Maybe you had some other reason to get rid of Curtis," she suggested. "Maybe he found out something about you that you didn't want anyone else to know."

Jane was trying to recall the details of what Guy Drummond had said about some new scandal involving Dennis.

"Found out something about me I didn't want anybody to know?" Dennis repeated with heavy sarcasm. "Like what? Whatever I do, I do right out in public where everybody can see it. You know something I've done, spit it out. If you don't know what you're talking about, shut your mouth. Otherwise, the *Washington Post* and its advertisers are going to find themselves the target of a boycott. My movement has a lot of members."

"We'll continue right after a news update, and a word from your local sponsors," Jerry announced.

The air was now so thick with anger and resentment that Jane felt she was suffocating. She had to get out for a few minutes while an anchorwoman in a tiny booth read the one A.M. news.

"Don't worry, I'll be back," she called over her shoulder.

"Don't bother," VanDyke shouted after her.

Jane called the *Post* and begged the night editor to save space for the revelation of Davenport's killer. She was sure someone would crack, she told the editor.

In the control room, K.T. was worried, too.

"You've lost momentum," the producer scolded her host. "You're letting them off the hook."

"What else am I supposed to do?" Jerry shouted.

Jane, back from the phone, listened to the bickering. The *Post* would surely fire her for taking part in this fiasco. She never should have gotten mixed up with Jerry Knight.

"Maybe none of them did it," Jerry said. "Maybe this was a bad idea."

"Don't panic," K.T. ordered, hopping off her chair. "A little something goes wrong and you go all to pieces. You lose it now, we're all in deep doodoo."

"This was your idea," Jerry said.

"And it will work," K.T. shot back. The tiny woman began pacing the narrow control room. "What made you think it was going to be easy? You think you ask a couple of tough questions, the murderer is all of a sudden going to admit everything to you? These are tough people. They've survived in Washington, haven't they? So you have to keep after them. Eventually, one of them is going to crack."

On the speakers, they heard the newscaster winding up her report. A station break, two minutes of commercials, and the *Night Talker* show would be back on the air.

"All right, all right. Listen." K.T. paced on her short legs. "Here's what you do: open up the phones. The lines are going crazy."

She motioned to the phone console.

"Let the listeners ask them questions for a while. There are a lot of nut cases out there, Jerry. Maybe one of them will say something so outrageous that the murderer will blurt out the truth."

"It's worth a shot," Jane agreed. "Maybe somebody who knows something will call, like Drummond did. Somebody somewhere knows something about why Curtis was killed. Maybe they'll call."

"Okay," Jerry decided. "We'll go to the phones after the break."

K.T. hopped back up into her chair at the producer's desk. Sammy tripped the theme-music tape. Jerry and Jane hurried back into the studio just as the announcer introduced the second hour of the *Night Talker* show.

"I'm back!" Jerry proclaimed when the microphone light came on. "A living legend, back with the most unusual show in the history of radio. We started off tonight talking about the environment. But now we're talking about a murder, the murder of Curtis Davies Davenport, right after he appeared on the *Night Talker* show. We're going to the phones right now so our listeners, the *real* people of America, can ask this panel *their* questions."

A computer screen in front of Jerry listed the first names of the callers, where they were calling from, and the phone line they were holding on. Jerry pushed a button on his phone console.

"Leonard in Davenport, Iowa, you're on the air," Jerry announced.

"Jerry?"

"Go ahead."

"Am I on the air?"

"You're on the air!"

"No kidding! I'm on the *Night Talker* show! Well, I think this is really a stupid show, Jerry. I mean, why don't you just let the cops find out who killed that guy? I mean, I'd rather hear you interviewing Julia Roberts than talking to these deadheads. I mean, it's boring—"

Jerry killed the call.

Jane looked at her watch. One-ten. Time was running out. She was finished at the *Post,* she was sure of that. Coming on this show to force a public confession out of Curtis's murderer had been idiotic. She was going to be a laughingstock.

"Les in Kansas City. You're on the air."

"I'm suspicious of that Jack . . . what's his name? Vanman?"

"VanDyke," Jerry corrected.

"Yeah, him. He says he was in Chicago at a political fund-raiser when that guy was killed. Right? But he wasn't killed until, like, what? After two in the morning? What fund-raiser runs that late? VanDyke could have flown back to Washington in a chartered jet and had time to kill that guy. Then he could have flown back to Chicago in the jet after the murder so in the morning everybody would think he was there all night. Whadaya think, Jerry?"

"Good theory, Les!" Jerry perked up. "What about it, Jack? Is the caller right?"

"The caller is a bigger schmuck than you are. Maybe your listeners have the same IQ you have, jerk, in the low double digits. So let me repeat myself so all your fans out there will be sure to catch my meaning: *I did not kill Davenport.*"

But the next caller, Diane in Tulsa, picked up on the theory. She suggested that Jerry check with the airports in the Washington area to see if a chartered jet from Chicago had landed in the hours before Davenport's murder.

And that's how it went for the next fifteen minutes, serious questions and suggestions aimed at unmasking the murderer, alternating with kook calls and demands that Jerry drop his amateur sleuthing in favor of more interesting topics like sports.

"The Night Talker returns right after these messages," Jerry announced at one-thirty.

His guests usually left at two A.M., so Jerry couldn't insist that these four stay longer. They wouldn't anyhow. They could justify marching out at two o'clock without arousing suspicion.

During the break, the four glared at Jerry. None spoke. Jerry studied the faces around the table one after the other as the commercials played through the speakers. Pat Howell on the host's left. Kurt Voss, her boyfriend, next to her. Then Jane Day. The giant Drake Dennis on Jane's left. And Jack VanDyke at Jerry's right side. Their faces showed only anger. Even Jane looked angry. He guessed she blamed him for dragging her into this embarrassing debacle. But, hey, he still had a half hour. It ain't over till it's over. He hadn't heard any fat lady singing yet.

The first caller after the break was Abe in Washington, D.C.

"I have a question for Mr. Dennis," the caller said.

Jerry thought the voice sounded familiar.

"Go ahead, caller. Ask your question."

"Mr. Dennis, are you still the captain of that softball team that plays around Washington? What do you call it? Big Machine? Something like that?"

"Please, caller, we are not doing sports tonight—" Wait a minute! Jerry recognized the voice. It was A. L. Jones, the detective. "But I'll let Drake answer your question."

Drake Dennis had no reason to suspect the caller was a detective. He answered the question eagerly, glad for the change of subject.

"Oh, yeah, the team's still playing. The Big Green Machine, in the Public Interest Softball League, over in West Potomac Park."

Jerry stayed out of it. Jane recognized the voice now, too.

"You still killing your opponents?" asked the deep voice on the phone.

"Killing them is right!" Dennis had dropped his guard. "We beat Common Cause ten to three. And we knocked off the National Organization for Women eighteen to one! They had three *men* playing for them and we still beat them!"

"Really bashing the opposition, huh?"

"You're not kidding, bashing them." Dennis was babbling, released from the tension of the past hour and a half. "How do you know about the Big Green Machine?"

"I'm in the D.C. Government Employees League," Jones explained. "We played you one time."

"Yeah? What team?"

"Homicide detectives. The Avenging Angels. We're always looking for guys who like to bash their opponents."

Drake Dennis's attitude changed abruptly.

"What's your fucking problem, man?" he demanded.

Sammy was so engrossed in the drama that he failed to activate the censor button. The word went out over the air.

"You're pretty good at bashing, huh?" the voice on the phone needled. "Are you good at bashing off the field, too? Like in parking garages?"

"Fuck!" Dennis snarled.

Sammy forgot the censor button again.

Dennis grabbed the backpack from under his chair, rummaged inside, and pulled out a hand grenade.

Pat Howell screamed. Kurt Voss ducked under the table. Jack VanDyke cursed. Jane pulled out her pad and started scribbling.

"Drake Dennis has just jumped up," Jerry said, giving the listeners a play-by-play account. "He's got a hand grenade in his left hand . . . Dennis is obviously the one who killed Curtis Davenport . . . Unmasked here live on the air by the Night Talker . . . Dennis is rushing to the door of the studio now . . . he's still got that hand grenade . . . He's at the door now . . . he opens it . . . Oh, my God! He's pulled the pin on—He's throwing it . . . Oh, shi—"

Listeners heard a loud bang, then silence.

Outside the studio, a door on the left gave entry to the control room. To the right was a corridor that Dennis remembered twisted its way back to the elevators. He turned right.

Detective A. L. Jones was crouched in the corridor, holding a gun in both hands, pointed directly at Drake Dennis.

"Police! Freeze, motherfucker! Move an inch, I'll blow your fucking head off! Drop that pack! Now!"

Dennis half turned, looking behind him for a route of escape.

"I said freeze, asshole! You've got three seconds to drop that pack and get your fucking hands over your head, or they're going to be cleaning your brains off the walls for a week! Do it, fucker!"

The huge bearded white man sized up the wild-eyed stubby black detective. Dennis dropped his pack and raised his hands.

"Lean against the wall! Hands high! Spread your legs, motherfucker! Move!"

Dennis followed the detective's instructions.

Jane Day emerged from a cloud of greasy smoke roiling out of the studio. She was hacking and wheezing. A putrid odor clung to her.

She took in the tableau of Jones and Dennis, but kept moving down the corridor toward the elevators.

"Are you going to charge him with Curtis's murder?" she called back over her shoulder.

"Yes," A.L. answered.

"How'd you know it was him?" Jane yelled.

"Found the murder weapon in his car trunk."

"What was it?" Jane was almost at the turn at the end of the corridor.

"A softball bat."

Jane disappeared around the corner in a flat run for the elevators.

"I'm going to make the final edition!" Jones heard her exclaim.

CHAPTER FIFTY-TWO

DRAKE DENNIS WAS facedown in the corridor, his wrists fastened behind him with a plastic tab, and the detective was on his walkie-talkie summoning help when Jerry Knight, Pat Howell, Jack VanDyke, and Kurt Voss stumbled out of the studio, gagging and hollering.

From the smell of them, Jones guessed the explosive device Drake Dennis had set off was a stink bomb or tear gas canister, frightening but harmless. No doubt left over from one of his environmental demonstrations.

Jerry staggered into the control room.

"We're off the air," he complained. "The greatest show of my life and we're off the air."

"I know it," K.T. snapped. "We're working on it."

As an afterthought, the producer asked, "You all right?"

"I'm okay, except I smell like shit. And I want to get back on the air!"

Howell, VanDyke, and Voss departed in outrage. Jerry

was assured he would be hearing from lawyers in the morning.

"Sammy, goddamn it!" K.T. prodded the technician.

By then Sammy had determined that the concussion from Dennis's stink bomb had damaged the equipment in Jerry's studio, but the rest of the network was still operating. He hurried Jerry and K.T. into another studio while other technicians made some patches and threw some switches. In a few minutes, the Night Talker was broadcasting again to his millions of fans.

The remaining three hours of the program was devoted to Talk Back, America, as usual. Most of the callers lauded Jerry for unmasking the murderer and exposing the environmental kooks.

"They think it's okay to kill people as long as they save the snail darter," was one of the milder comments.

But a few listeners protested that Jerry had sunk to a new low in his vendetta against environmentalists, falsely accusing Drake Dennis, a dedicated savior of planet Earth. Dennis was a pacifist, they said, incapable of such an act. Jerry had better watch his own step when he walked out of the studio at dawn, one pacifist warned.

One caller asked Jerry to find out who had killed Marilyn Monroe.

And one caller, whom Jerry recognized as Guy Drummond, said simply "Thank you," and hung up.

CHAPTER FIFTY-THREE

Jane was lucky. An empty cab was cruising M Street in front of the ATN studios just as she ran out the door. She instructed the driver to make a left at Twenty-fourth Street and another left at L. From there it was a straight shot, nine blocks, to the *Post*.

Jane looked at her watch. At most she'd have thirty minutes to write her story. The old newspaper adage had it that it took longer to write a short story than a long one. Tonight, she didn't have time for conciseness. She'd just do a straight recitation of the facts in the old-fashioned, almost outmoded, inverted-pyramid style. She'd get the color and polish, the anecdotes and her own reactions, into the follow-ups. Undoubtedly, there would be follow-ups.

The driver turned left onto Fifteenth Street, made a fast U-turn, and they were in front of the *Post*. Jane threw a five-dollar bill at him and didn't wait for change. She sprinted into the lobby, waved her plastic ID badge at the security guard, and dove into an elevator.

The huge expanse of newsroom on the fifth floor was almost deserted. At that hour, only two or three people were at work in what seemed like an acre of desks and cubicles under the low fluorescent-light ceiling.

Jane ran to the desk of the late night editor, Jeff Plotnick. She was breathless from running, and from excitement.

"Drake Dennis . . . just arrested . . . Curtis's murder . . . on Jerry Knight show . . ."

"Don't waste time telling me," Plotnick instructed. "I heard it on the radio. Great story. Here's a cassette, cued to where Dennis blows. Go write. Fast."

He handed her a tape.

Jane hurried toward her computer terminal, back among the deserted desks of the Metro section police reporters. Maybe she'd be moving to a more prestigious part of the newsroom now, she hoped.

"Two hundred words," Plotnick called after her. "No more. You've got twenty-five minutes. Nothing fancy."

Plotnick was sixty, short, with a potbelly, pasty skin, and a few strands of limp hair crisscrossing his head. He was never going to be one of the *Post*'s big-name editors. But five nights a week he was entrusted with updating the final edition of one of America's most important newspapers when news broke late and almost everyone else had gone home. Forty years of work at the anonymous editing desks of journalism had taught him how to handle these late-night crises in a steady and professional manner. He took pride in his specialized talent.

In exactly twenty-five minutes, Jane sent a signal to

Plotnick's computer terminal. She had finished her story. It was ready for him to edit and send to the press room.

There was nothing else for Jane to do now, except hang around to answer any last-minute questions from Jeff, then wait for the final edition to come off the presses.

She leaned back in her chair and felt tears welling in her eyes. She had redeemed her career at the *Post*. The tears began to roll down her cheeks. The killer of her friend Curtis had been caught. Now she cried openly and hard. She had lived after feeling certain in the studio she was going to die.

When the tears stopped, Jane fixed her makeup. Soon a news assistant arrived with the first copies of the final edition.

She held the paper, which exuded the smell of ink and cheap pulp newsprint. There it was, top of the page, above the fold.

Murder Suspect Nabbed During Radio Show

Dennis, 'Green' Leader, Held In Davenport Killing

By Jane Day

WASHINGTON POST STAFF WRITER

Washington, D.C.—Police early today arrested environmental activist Drake Dennis for the brutal murder of clean-air crusader Curtis Davies Davenport after a dramatic confrontation broadcast live on an all-night radio talk show.

After being tricked into making incriminating statements during a broadcast of the *Night Talker* program on the All Talk Network, Dennis set off an explosive device in the studio in an effort to escape. But he was arrested in a corridor outside the studio by veteran D.C. homicide detective A. L. Jones.

Dennis's motive in the alleged murder was not immediately known. Jones told the *Post* the murder weapon was—

"Nice job." Plotnick interrupted her reading. "Keep this up, you could become a halfway decent reporter."

"Thanks."

CHAPTER FIFTY-FOUR

THERE WAS NO way Jane could go home and go to sleep. She was too wired.

She thought about calling her mother. But it was too late, even in California. She thought about calling Russ Williamson and gloating, but that probably wouldn't be a smart career move.

She couldn't think of one friend, man or woman, who would be pleased to be awakened to share her excitement.

The last police reporter had departed. Even Jeff was getting ready to leave for his home in—where? McLean? Kensington? Some suburb for couples.

The biggest night of her career, and no one to celebrate with.

The only sound in the *Post* newsroom was the hum of the fluorescent lights.

Jane felt alone.

She looked at her watch. Four-thirty in the morning.

The only person she knew who was up at four-thirty was Jerry Knight. She decided to return to the studio.

She walked across the street to the Madison Hotel and climbed into a waiting cab. She was going back to gather details for tomorrow's story, she tried to convince herself.

Just as Jane arrived at the ATN building, A. L. Jones pulled up in his dirty vanilla detective's car.

"Yo," he called to her. "Got your story written?"

"Yep. Got your murderer booked?"

"Yeah."

The elevator doors slid open to a chaotic scene. The ATN offices were swarming with TV camera crews, news photographers, reporters, policemen in uniform, policemen in blue jeans and sweatshirts lettered POLICE across the back, and detectives with badges flopping out of the breast pockets of rumpled suits.

She followed close behind Jones as he pushed through the crowd. The corridor where Dennis had been captured was cordoned off with yellow tape imprinted POLICE LINE DO NOT CROSS.

Jones scuttled down another hallway. After a couple of turns they were at the control room. K.T. and Sammy looked up and nodded when they entered.

Jerry Knight's closing monologue was blaring from the speakers.

". . . greatest show in the history of radio. And you can tell your grandchildren you heard it. Jerry Knight uncovers a murderer live on the air! And a very brave member of the D.C. Homicide squad, Detective Abraham Lincoln Jones, stops him from getting away. I know, it comes as a shock to my loyal fans to hear me say anything nice about the D.C. police department. But, hey, I give credit where credit is due."

Jane glanced at Detective Jones. He was grinning.

K.T. sliced her right index finger across her throat, the signal for Jerry to wrap it up.

"I'm afraid we're out of time, ladies and gentlemen. You'll just have to live without me for two entire days. I know, it won't be easy. But I will return Monday at midnight, a modern knight armored in true wisdom, going forth yet again to combat the forces of political correctness and big-brother government, puncturing the windbags, deflating the self-important, exposing the bureaucrats who spend your money on dumb programs, putting an end to bull once and for all. And now, *certifiable* upholder of law and order! Good night from the Night Talker. God bless you and God bless freedom."

The theme music swelled to a crescendo. A recorded announcer's voice intoned that Jerry Knight's opinions did not necessarily represent the views of ATN or its advertisers.

The host bounded into the control room.

"Yes!" he exclaimed. "Let's see Larry King top this!"

K.T. gave Jerry a congratulatory hug, then she and Sammy left the control room to contend with the tumult outside.

CHAPTER FIFTY-FIVE

K NIGHT LIT UP his morning cigar early to celebrate.

"If I'd known you were going to say something nice about the police department like that, I'd of told my friends to listen in," A. L. Jones rumbled in his gravelly voice.

"Credit where credit is due," Jerry repeated.

"Still, you never should of done what you did," the detective admonished. "You're a lucky man. If that dude had been packing a piece, he'd of popped you. You'd be dead right now. They'd be looking for a new Night Talker."

"I'm glad you were here," Jerry said in a subdued tone.

"Make your deadline?" Jerry asked Jane.

"I had twenty-five minutes to write two hundred words. Page one."

"Didja spell my name right?"

"It's 'L-A-R-R-Y K-I-N-G,' right?"

"I like a girl with a sense of humor." Knight reached out and squeezed her hand. Jane pulled a notebook from her tapestry shoulder bag and ostentatiously fanned away the smoke from his cigar.

She sat down at the producer's desk.

"How'd you know it was Drake Dennis?" she asked A.L.

"I didn't know for sure," he replied. "But after I ran background checks on all the suspects in the computer, I had a pretty strong idea it was him."

He eased his stumpy body into Sammy's deserted chair at the technician's console.

"Turns out Dennis was convicted of blowing up an ROTC office at the University of Wisconsin back in the seventies when he was into the antiwar thing," the detective explained. "Got out in eighteen months. Another time, few years ago, cops found dynamite in the trunk of his car. On his way to blow up some fishing boats he didn't think should be catching dolphins, some kind of environmental shit like that."

"Did he serve time for that?" Jane asked, taking notes.

"Nah," Jones replied in disgust. "Got himself a smart lawyer and got off 'cause the cops didn't have a search warrant to look in his trunk. Damn bleeding-heart judges. No wonder we can't keep the criminals in jail."

"Maybe we're not so far apart after all," Jerry commented approvingly.

"Anyhow, computer says the dude knows something about explosives, so I figured he's the one tried to blow up your car, Mr. Night Talker. And I figured whoever tried to blow up your car was the one dropped Davenport and was trying to get you because he thought you was onto him."

Jerry puffed his cigar.

"Turns out Dennis put the bomb in your car 'cause he was pissed at you for giving publicity to Davenport instead of him," Jones continued. "Says he was just scaring you, not trying to kill you. If he'd wanted to kill you, he would have made a bigger bomb."

"Couple of old arrests for dynamite, that's all that made you think Drake Dennis killed Curtis?" Jane asked.

"You got a low opinion of cops, too, huh?" the detective said. "While Dennis was on the air, I took a look in the trunk of his car down in the garage."

"With a search warrant?" the reporter needled.

"Give it a rest, will you?" Jones snapped.

"What did you find in his trunk?" Jane asked. "More dynamite?"

"Nah. Softball equipment. Gloves. Balls. And a canvas bag full of bats. One of the bats had stains on it could of been blood. It looks like the green paint on the bat matches some paint chips found on Davenport's head," Jones reported. "Ain't confirmed, but looks like it."

"The murder weapon," Jerry said. "And that's when you phoned the show and started questioning Dennis."

"Yeah. I came up here, used the phone in that office right there. Figured you'd been at it almost two hours and weren't getting any of 'em to confess. Thought I'd see if a real detective could do any better."

"You really didn't know for sure that Dennis was the murderer when you made that call?" Jane prodded. "You were just seeing what his reaction would be when you talked about 'bashing' opponents?"

"That's right. And it worked."

The detective flashed Jerry a satisfied grin, intended to be the last word in their debate over the quality of law enforcement in Washington.

"But what if Dennis had been carrying a gun?" Jane persisted. "Or if that stink bomb thing had been a real hand grenade?"

"Welcome to real life, Miss Washington Post," Jones told her. "To you, this deal was a story for the newspaper. To him"—nodding at Jerry—"it was some kind of publicity thing to make him look like a hero to the nut cases out there listening to him. To me, this is what I'm into every day and every night."

"Did Dennis say why he killed Curtis?" Jane asked in a quiet voice.

"Oh, yeah, he told it all," Jones said. "First he called up one of them downtown lawyers, came into Homicide huffing and puffing about habeas corpus and Miranda rulings, all that lawyer shit. We got him cooled down and Dennis just spilled it all out. Seems that Dennis was taking money from that company . . . what's the name? The one gave a hundred thousand bucks to that senator?"

"Z-Chem Plastics," Jane offered.

"Yeah. Dennis was taking money from them—"

"For what?"

"—for not doing one of his environmental protest things against them. He told them he was going to organize a consumer boycott against them if they didn't kick in twenty thou a month. And they were paying it."

"That must have been the 'deal' Drummond told Davenport about in the phone call," Jerry said.

Jane was sickened by such a cynical betrayal of a movement she and Curtis had believed in.

"It goes on all the time," Jerry said. "Civil rights organizations. Environmental organizations. Ethnic groups. Women's groups. They all do it. They ask big companies to make a donation to their 'education' fund or their 'legal defense' fund. A 'scholarship' fund. Nothing overt, just an implied promise that if the company makes a contribution, the organization won't make trouble for them."

Jane turned back to the detective. "So . . .?"

"Dennis was listening the night Davenport was on the *Night Talker* show. Heard Davenport say something that made him think Davenport was going to blow the whistle on him."

Jane tried to remember Curtis's words on the tape. He'd talked about Corporate America making payoffs to politicians. That was clearly a reference to Jacobsen.

But she recalled he'd said something else, something about payoffs to people who claimed they believed in the environmental movement. It hadn't meant anything to her the first time she'd heard it.

But Drake Dennis must have heard it and assumed Curtis was talking about the money he was extorting from Z-Chem.

"Dennis rushed over here and waited for Davenport in the garage," Jones continued. "Dennis confronted him when he came down from the show. Offered to split the payoff money with him if Davenport kept quiet about it. Davenport said he wouldn't, so Dennis beat his head in—"

Jane gasped. The detective looked at her and didn't finish the sentence.

"Hard to believe Dennis would kill Davenport over something like that," Jerry commented.

"Oh, it was more than keeping Davenport from exposing him," Jones explained. "He hated Davenport. Jealous of him for getting so much publicity. Dennis wanted the publicity for himself. You should of heard him telling about it. Every time Davenport was on the *Today* show or CNN talking about some environmental shit, Dennis went nuts. Couldn't stand the competition. And when it looked like Davenport was going to ruin him, he just totally lost it and busted him."

"I'm glad you got him," Jane said.

"Yeah. Got both of 'em."

"Both?" Jerry asked.

"Got Dennis for doing Davenport. And he gave up Kurt Voss for passing the money from . . . Z-Chem, whatever it is. U.S. Attorney is trying to figure out what to book him on right now."

"Figures," Jane said. "Voss is the lobbyist for Z-Chem, so makes sense he'd be the one paying off Dennis."

"And paying off VanDyke, too," Jones added.

"VanDyke?" Jane was puzzled. "VanDyke was taking money, too?"

"The hundred thou to that center went through VanDyke," Jones reported.

"But Jacobsen knew about it, right?" Jane asked.

"Don't think so," the detective replied. "Nobody mentioned him. Looks clean to me."

"He can't be!" Jane protested. She remembered VanDyke had accepted full responsibility at the news conference. But nobody had believed him.

"Innocent until proven guilty," Jerry needled her. "Or don't you liberals believe in that?"

"What about Pat Howell?" Jane asked the detective. "Is she dealing drugs on the Hill?"

"If she is, we ain't caught her at it," Jones responded. "But if somebody drops a brick of snow in her car Thursday lunchtime, we'll be watching."

The walkie-talkie hooked to the detective's belt crackled an indecipherable message.

"Say again."

A.L. put the radio to his ear.

"That's me," Jones told Jerry and Jane. "I gotta go."

"What is it?" asked Jane, ever the reporter.

"Dude got mad, shot up a dance place on Florida Avenue. Couple of people wasted."

Jane reached out and shook the detective's stubby hand. Jerry did the same.

"Maybe your side of town is meaner than my side of town, Mr. Night Talker," the detective said. "At least on my side, I know which ones are the good guys and which ones are the bad guys."

A. L. Jones hurried out of the control room.

CHAPTER FIFTY-SIX

So, WHAT ARE you going to do now?" Jerry asked Jane when they were alone.

"Right now? I'm going home and go to bed. Then I'm going to get up and go into the *Post* and get my ass chewed out again for the mistake on Jacobsen. I can't understand it. Curtis told me it was the senator who personally took the hundred thousand dollars. He was very certain about it."

"You were used," Jerry said, not unsympathetically. "Most reporters who accept leaks are used. Somebody wants to settle an old score, do in a rival, destroy some legislation, they leak a negative story. And usually the story is too good to check. The reporter doesn't *want* to find out if there's another side to it, or that it's flat-out wrong. Too good to check. Nasty little secret in journalism."

"But why would Curtis want to deliberately hurt Jacobsen?"

"Who knows?" Jerry shrugged. "Pay him back for holding up some legislation the environmentalists want? Weaken his influence? Probably to derail his presidential hopes. I don't think Davenport wanted a conservative in the White House."

"Curtis was a good person," Jane insisted.

"Maybe so," Jerry said. "But Washington turns good people bad. You've got to be bad to play the game here."

"He had principles," she insisted, reluctant to believe her friend had been just another player corrupted by the Washington game. "He stood by his principles right to the end. Dennis tried to buy his silence, and he refused."

"In Washington, when you stand up for your principles, it usually costs you your job," Jerry said. "In Davenport's case, it cost him his life."

She stared into the empty studio.

"Want to go out for some breakfast?" Jerry asked.

"I thought you don't do breakfast."

"I don't do *lunch*. And you don't do dinner, so breakfast is the only meal we have in common."

"We've got *nothing* in common. We're as different as night and day."

She realized her play on words and laughed despite herself.

"Night and day meet at dawn," Jerry said. "It's dawn. Let's go to breakfast."

"You are a jerk."

"I'm going to assume that's a 'yes.' "